PRAISE FOR

◆ ◆ ◆

"Shana Norris has brilliantly recast the entire ensemble of
Homer's *Iliad* to fit the contemporary setting in her novel. . . .
Readers will be seduced by the watchful observer, Cassie,
who narrates the story with a simple honesty and takes you
page by page into this vengeful tale of pride, love, and glory."
—*ALAN*

"While *The Iliad* story line lends richness to the narrative,
the book stands alone, and readers unfamiliar with the classic
will still enjoy the war between high schools, started over a
beautiful girl." —*School Library Journal*

"Norris's prose is breezy, and playful references to
the *Iliad* entertain." —*Publishers Weekly*

◆ ◆ ◆

• • •

ALSO BY SHANA NORRIS

Something to Blog About

• • •

SHANA NORRIS

AMULET BOOKS
NEW YORK

PUBLISHER'S NOTE: This is a work of fiction. Names, characters, places, and incidents
are either the product of the author's imagination or are used fictitiously, and any
resemblance to actual persons, living or dead, business establishments, events, or locales
is entirely coincidental.

The Library of Congress has cataloged the original edition of this book as follows:

Norris, Shana.
Troy High / by Shana Norris.
p. cm.
Summary: Best friends Cassie and Greg get caught in the middle of a decades-old football
rivalry between their high school teams, the Spartans and the Trojans, in this novel loosely
based on Homer's classic tale, the Iliad.
ISBN 978-0-8109-4647-7
[1. Competition (Psychology)—Fiction. 2. Best friends—Fiction. 3. Friendship—Fiction.
4. Football—Fiction. 5. High schools—Fiction. 6. Schools—Fiction.] I. Title.

Paperback ISBN: 978-0-8109-9665-6

PZ7.N7984Tro 2009
[Fic]—dc22
2008046182

Copyright © 2009 Shana Norris
Book design by Maria T. Middleton

Printed and bound in U.S.A.
10 9 8 7 6 5 4 3

Amulet Books are available at special discounts when purchased in quantity for premiums and
promotions as well as fundraising or educational use. Special editions can also be created to
specification. For details, contact specialmarkets@abramsbooks.com or the address below.

ABRAMS
THE ART OF BOOKS SINCE 1949
115 West 18th Street
New York, NY 10011
www.abramsbooks.com

For my grandparents,
Charles and Mary Thomas
and
Jimmie and Georgia Hudler

I THINK THERE IS NO ONE OF MEN
WHO HAS ESCAPED FATE, NEITHER THE
COWARD NOR THE BRAVE MAN,
AFTER HE HAS ONCE BEEN BORN.

— Homer, *The Iliad*

1

IT WAS A LATE SUNDAY AFTERNOON WHEN I kissed my best friend.

We had been playing our favorite video game, Martial Battle 2, in his parents' den. Playing video games was something we did a lot. Kissing was not.

"Oh, you are *so* dead, Cassie Prince," Greg Mennon growled, his eyes locked on the TV screen.

We watched as the two fighters on the screen lunged toward each other. My fighter, a woman dressed in a long flowing gown, grabbed Greg's hulking fighter and slung him over her shoulder. He fell so hard, he cracked the virtual floor. The screen proclaimed, CASSIE WINS!

"That's what you think," I said, kicking Greg's foot with my own. "I even beat you in heels."

"You cheat," Greg told me.

I snorted. "Yeah, okay. If it makes you feel any better, go ahead and believe that I cheat and not that you just suck."

Greg hit the button on his controller to start a new game and the Choose a Character screen appeared.

"So tomorrow's the big day," he said as he selected his next fighter. "We go back to being enemies again."

I rolled my eyes. "I can hardly wait."

Every school had a bit of a rivalry with other schools, but the one between Lacede High and Troy High was legendary. It made sense, I suppose, that our mascots were the Spartans and Trojans, respectively. Just as the Greeks and Trojans battled thousands of years ago, our schools fought wars on the football field.

The rivalry had been going on since before my parents had been in high school. Back in the 1950s, right after Troy High was built, Lacede and Troy played their first football game against each other. The game took place at Lacede and everything was going fine—until the fourth quarter. Then a Trojan player caught the ball just before being roughly shoved out of bounds by a Spartan. Or at least, that's the Trojan version of the story. The Spartans claim that the Trojan had already stepped out of bounds before he caught the ball. The Trojan shoved the Spartan back and the coaches had to break them up so the game could continue. The referee sided with the Spartans.

But that wasn't the end of it. The next time the Trojans lined up to start their offensive play, one of the Spartans said the Trojans played football like little girls and they should try cheerleading instead. The quarterback leaped out of position to lunge at the Spartan and wrestle him to the ground. Soon, all of the players, even the ones who had been sitting on the sidelines at the time, were throwing punches at one another. And a bloody brawl ensued.

Troy lost the game, the Trojan quarterback was banned from the team for the rest of the season, and war between the schools had been declared. During my parents' time at Troy, some guys had let a bunch of pigs loose during a dance at Lacede. In revenge, the Spartans had rigged up buckets of soured milk to dump onto the Trojans when they entered the school one morning.

The rivalry was a thing of legend around the two neighboring school districts. Everyone had a story. Everyone liked to act as if they played a part in continuing the saga.

Greg went to Lacede High.

I went to Troy.

Greg pressed the Start button and our fighters appeared onscreen again, staring at each other while the countdown flashed between them.

I punched at the buttons on my controller, making my fighter throw a wild series of punches and kicks so fast that Greg could barely get his fighter out of the way in time.

"Twenty bucks says Lacede kicks Troy's butt this season," Greg grunted as his fingers tried to keep up with mine.

My dancing lady tried to grab Greg's blue wolverine, but he jumped out of the way at the last second, flying over her head to land behind her and grab her around the waist. The wolverine swung the dancing lady over his head, but I got her to free herself and somersault through the air, then land gracefully.

I rolled my eyes. "You know I think that rivalry is stupid, but there is no way Lacede will beat Troy. You haven't seen Perry and Hunter practicing."

Perry and Hunter were my older brothers and both played on the Troy High football team, Hunter as the quarterback and Perry a cornerback.

"And you haven't seen Lucas," Greg told me. His older brother was the Lacede quarterback.

His fighter grabbed mine again, but this time she

couldn't break the hold. He tossed the dancing lady backward, slamming her into the ground.

Greg punched the air with his fists. "Booyah! Who sucks now?"

I threw my controller at him. "Grow up. It's just a game."

"Aw, what's wrong?" Greg taunted me. "Sad now that you lost? What happened to all those big words about how you can kick my butt in heels?"

I bopped Greg over the head with a throw pillow. "Shut up."

"Wanna play again?" he asked.

"I'm tired," I said, leaning back into the couch.

"No, you're scared." He poked a finger into my ribs. "Scared of being beat again."

"Puh-leeze . . . ," I said, swatting his hand away.

But Greg wouldn't give up easily. "You're scared of wounding your pride. Every time you start to lose, you claim you're tired." He leaned toward me, smirking. "Admit it, Cassie. You're just scared. You've never done a thing in your life that frightens you."

"Oh, really?" I asked, suddenly filled with annoyance and the desire to prove him wrong.

For months I had thought about kissing Greg, had even dreamed about it. But I'd always been too afraid to do it, too afraid of ruining our friendship.

We'd met two years ago at band camp, when Greg had discovered me hiding in a supply closet and scarfing down three pints of chocolate-chip-cookie-dough ice cream stolen from the counselors' freezer while everyone else watched the evening movie. I had planned to share it with my roommates in the hopes that maybe they'd stop calling me Gassie. Which they had started doing on our first night at band camp, when I accidentally laughed so hard that, well, you can guess what happened.

But then as I had headed back to my room with the stolen ice cream, I'd overheard my roommates laughing about me with some other girls in the common room.

So I hid in the supply closet and started eating all of the ice cream myself. I was halfway through the third pint when the door opened and Greg came in, looking for a soft rag to clean his trumpet with.

I had seen Greg around camp before then, but I could never work up the courage to talk to him. Not only was he a Spartan—even in band camp Spartans and Trojans didn't mingle together—but also other people always surrounded him because he was so nice and friendly. And I . . . well, before Greg, my last best friend had moved away when I was ten and I'd just never really gotten along with anyone else. It didn't help that my brother Perry liked to tease me in school in front of everyone. The rest of Troy

High followed his lead just because they thought he was so cool.

Now, the supply closet was pretty roomy, but I was not thrilled at having company. Just as I was about to hurl a spoonful of ice cream at Greg's face in the hopes of getting him to go away and leave me alone, he took the carton from me, helped himself to a big spoonful, and somehow made me laugh.

We'd been inseparable ever since, even though our schools were the biggest rivals in the area. Unfortunately, we had to endure constant harassment about being friends.

But still, the thought of being *more* than friends had popped into my head only recently. And once it did, it would *not* go away. And believe me, I tried to force it away by thinking about things like Greg sick with a snotty nose. But even that wouldn't get rid of those crazy thoughts.

So I leaned across the distance between us on the faded green couch and planted my lips on his before I could change my mind. Never would I have dared do it if Greg hadn't taunted me like that.

I was kissing my best friend.

The guy who had seen me with bed head and dressed in my grungy pajamas.

I was kissing Greg.

And I liked it.

I pulled back, keeping my eyes on the wall in front of me. Greg still hadn't moved. Shocked, he sat perfectly still, his controller pinched in his hands.

I heard the front door open and a moment later, Greg's older brother, Lucas, entered the room, followed by his girlfriend, Elena Argos, and his friend Owen, who was also on the Lacede football team.

"I'm not done talking to you, Lucas," Elena said, her hands on her hips.

"Well, I'm done listening." Lucas plopped onto the other end of the couch and snatched up the controller I had thrown at Greg. "Who wants to play me?"

I glanced at Greg from the corner of my eye. He still sat frozen.

Lucas waved his hand in front of his brother's face. "What's up with you? We playing or not?"

Greg snapped out of his stupor and tossed his controller to the floor. "No way. You cheat."

"Aw, poor wittle Gwegowy scared of a challenge?" Lucas asked, poking out his lower lip.

"I'll play," Owen said, scooping up the controller and squeezing onto the couch between Greg and me.

Elena glared down at Lucas with her dark blue eyes.

"If you have nothing better to do than play video games, I'm going home."

"See ya," Lucas called, not looking away from the TV.

I glanced at Elena to distract myself from the fact that *I had just kissed my best friend.* Elena was a sophomore, like me, while Lucas and his friends were juniors.

Two things made the Lacede-Troy rivalry even more heated this year: One, my brother Hunter had brought down the star of Lacede's defensive line—a wild card named Ackley—in the game between our two schools the year before. Not only did that secure the win for Troy in that particular game, but also since it was early in the season and Ackley had twisted his ankle pretty badly, he was unable to play in any of Lacede's remaining games that year. Therefore, Lacede had no chance at winning the regional championship. Lacede held Hunter responsible. And they were out to get him.

The second reason the rivalry had grown so huge this year was that over the summer the board of education had redrawn the school district lines to help ease overcrowding at Lacede. Which meant that some of the Lacede students would now be attending Troy High, starting tomorrow.

And the most beautiful girl at Lacede, Elena Argos, was one of those students.

My stomach twisted just a little at the thought of Elena

being set loose among the guys at Troy High. That couldn't lead to anything good. She was the kind of girl who could really drive guys crazy.

Elena looked over at me. "I don't know how you can stand to be around these immature little *boys* all day while they play video games, Cassie," she told me.

None of the guys seemed to hear her. Or else they were ignoring her.

"Uh," I said, removing myself from the couch and Greg's presence, "I'm going to . . . get something to drink."

"Bring me a Coke," Lucas said.

"Me too," Owen piped up as his fingers flew over the game controller.

Greg stared at the TV, his face a slight tinge of pink, and didn't say a word.

I jumped from the couch and practically dashed into the kitchen. I leaned against the counter for a moment, taking a long, deep breath.

What had I done? I had to be the stupidest, most insane—

"Can you believe what a jerk Lucas can be?" said a voice behind me.

I turned to see Elena had followed me into the kitchen. She stood with her arms crossed and her face creased into a dark scowl. She was even gorgeous when she was angry.

I busied myself with getting a glass of water. After taking a long sip, I said, "Why are you with him if he's a jerk?"

Elena snorted. "Good question." She sighed. "Take it from me, Cassie. Guys are nothing but giant pains. At least you got the nice Mennon brother."

I nearly dropped the glass I held and sputtered water down my chin. "W-what? I don't . . . Greg's not . . ."

"I had hoped that Lucas might one day grow up and stop being such a self-centered baby, but apparently that'll never happen," Elena went on, as if she didn't hear my stammering. "I could dump him right now and he'd never even notice because he's too busy playing video games." She raised her fists in front of her, shook them, and gave a growl of frustration.

I followed her back to the den, where the boys still sat in front of the TV.

"I'm leaving," Elena announced in a loud voice.

No one seemed to hear her. Lucas's and Owen's fighters battled onscreen, and Greg still stared blankly at the TV.

Elena glared at Lucas a moment longer, but he didn't seem to notice the death-ray look she shot him. Finally, Elena gave an aggravated groan, spun on her heel, and stomped out of the room. I heard the front door slam shut behind her.

The guys still sat on the couch, oblivious.

"You are so dead," Lucas said. He was an active player, swinging and tilting the controller while he punched the buttons and bounced in his seat.

I sneaked a few glances at Greg while Owen and Lucas battled. What was Greg thinking? Was he thinking about the fact that we had just kissed? Was he ever going to speak to me again? Was he going to pretend nothing happened?

I had to get out of there before I drove myself insane. Greg obviously thought it was a huge mistake. I could take the hint.

"I'll see you guys later," I said, standing up. "I'm going home."

"You want me to ride with you?" Greg asked.

I knew he would have gone with me if I had said yes, but I didn't want the ride to be one long, uncomfortable moment of silence.

"No, it's okay. See you later."

"Bye," Greg and Owen called as I left the room. I didn't think Lucas even noticed what went on outside of the video game.

I lifted my face toward the late summer sun as I rode my bike away from Greg's house. I couldn't believe how fast the summer had disappeared and how it was time to go back to school already.

School was not my favorite place in the world. Sure, I was in the Troy High band and I really did enjoy playing flute. But the rest of high school—the cliques, the popularity contests, the gossip—I was not a fan of.

Halfway home, a car horn beeped behind me. I turned and watched as the red Toyota slowed to a stop.

"Need a ride?" my brother Hunter asked, leaning out the passenger window.

I looked in the backseat, surprised to see it empty. Perry and Hunter usually had a carload of their friends riding around town with them. Or at least, as many as could fit into the beat-up car that they shared.

"Sure," I said.

Hunter got out and helped me put my bike into the trunk. Then just as I reached out to grab the door handle to get in, the car moved forward two feet.

"Perry, stop it," I said. I reached for the handle again, but once more Perry let off the brake and made the car lurch forward.

"Seriously, stop," Hunter said.

"I'm just playing," Perry insisted. He grinned at me as I climbed into the backseat. "Cassie knows that. Don't you, Cass?"

"Yeah, you're *so* hilarious," I muttered.

As we rode on toward home, Perry and Hunter talked

about the game coming up that weekend against Clark High. I watched them as they spoke, studied their hand gestures and facial expressions. They both looked casual and relaxed, as if being cool came naturally to them. And maybe it did. Maybe they got all the genes that made people popular, so there were none left for me when I came along.

How could I be the younger sister of the two most popular guys at Troy High and yet be a complete social outcast?

"So, Cass," Perry said, looking at me in the rearview mirror, "been at that Spartan's house again?"

I refused to meet his gaze and instead looked out at the passing houses. "He has a name."

"I hope he doesn't have any crazy ideas about Lacede beating us this season," Perry said, ignoring my response. "We'll fertilize the field with Spartan remains, just like we did last year. Right, Hunter?"

Hunter grunted in response.

"Actually, I've heard the Spartans have a pretty good team this year," I said, just to annoy Perry. He talked big before every game. "Ackley's ankle is good as new, and it sounds like he's out for blood after what happened last year."

Perry scowled and his knuckles tightened around

the steering wheel. "Just wait and see. We'll destroy the Spartans, especially your little boyfriend."

My neck flamed and I snapped, "He's not my boyfriend! And Greg doesn't even play sports."

"Lay off her, Perry," Hunter told him. "Save it for the football field."

"Oh, I will," Perry said. "The Spartans will never forget us."

2

"TROJANS RULE!" PERRY SHOUTED, PUMPING A fist into the air.

My brother had climbed onto the statue that stood outside the Troy High gymnasium, to the delight of his fans—cheerleaders, mostly, who all giggled up at him. The statue of a Trojan warrior sitting atop a horse stood in the courtyard in front of the gym. The Trojan wore armor just like paintings I'd seen in Greek mythology books: a helmet with a tall horsehair plume rising from the top. The Troy High band uniform featured a hat made to look like a Trojan warrior's helmet with ratty red and black feathers. Oh, yeah, it wasn't embarrassing at *all* to be seen dressed like that.

Hunter didn't even glance at Perry as he said, "Get down before you break your neck."

Perry sat behind the Trojan, on the back of the horse. "You ruin all my fun," he complained.

"Don't fall," Kelsey, a cheerleader, screeched, sounding as if she was terrified Perry would fall to his death from a height of four feet off the ground.

I sat nearby, on a bench along the brick path around the courtyard. All the most popular students hung out in the courtyard before classes each morning.

I was only allowed to sit in the vicinity because I was related to Perry and Hunter. If it weren't for the luck of birth, I would have been forced to the losers' circle—otherwise known as the front hall of the main building—with everyone else not worthy enough for the courtyard.

On second thought, I probably wouldn't even be welcome in the losers' circle. The geniuses were too smart for me and the average kids thought I was too smart for them.

So the only reason I sat in the courtyard was because everyone there pretty much ignored me and left me alone.

Well, everyone except Perry.

Perry had slid off the horse and survived—to the delight of Kelsey, I was sure. I didn't see him making his way toward me until he thumped the back of the book I pretended to read.

"You always have your nose stuck in some book," Perry said.

"Some of us like to expand our minds," I told him.

Perry snatched the book from me and read the title. *"Dueling with Desire,"* he said, raising his eyebrows.

He said it in a loud enough voice that it caught the attention of several people sitting nearby. My face grew hot as they all looked our way.

"Give me that," I said, snatching the book back and shoving it into my backpack.

"Do Mom and Dad know what kind of books you read?" Perry asked, giving me and his captive audience that stupid grin of his. "Aren't you a little young to be reading anything with the word 'desire' in the title?"

Laughter filled the air around us.

"Maybe she's trying to experience romance through a book," Kelsey said. "Since she hasn't had any in real life."

I looked up at Perry, pleading silently with him to be my brother, to stand up for my honor.

But I knew he wouldn't. That wasn't Perry's style. He favored his reputation over anything else.

"Lay off her," Hunter said in his deep, gruff voice. Immediately, the courtyard fell silent. The birds stopped chirping in the trees overhead, as if even they listened to anything Hunter Prince had to say.

"I'm just having a little fun," Perry said, shrugging. He turned away and headed back toward Kelsey and her friends.

I didn't look at anyone as I gathered up my things and walked away as fast as I could, my cheeks still burning with embarrassment.

Would it kill them to be nice to me? To let me be a part of their group? You would think maybe someone would want to be my friend just because of my brothers. But no, I couldn't even manage to get someone to use me to get closer to them.

The warning bell rang and I headed toward my first class, English.

"Cassie!" a voice called when I walked into the room. Elena Argos sat near the back, waving at me as if we were the best of friends.

I looked behind me to make sure there wasn't another Cassie standing nearby.

"Hi!" Elena said when I forced myself to walk toward her. "You're in this class?"

I nodded. "Mr. Sale's English class, right?" I asked, to make sure I hadn't stumbled into a parallel dimension.

"Yep." Elena gestured toward the seat in front of her. "Sit down."

I sat, feeling a little dazed.

"I'm so glad to see you," Elena said. "I was afraid I wouldn't know anyone in any of my classes. But thankfully, you came in!" She smiled wide at me. "You don't know how relieved I am to see a friendly face."

Was she serious?

"I heard only about fifty Lacede kids got sent to Troy," Elena told me. "The rest of the redistricted kids got sent to Sunset High."

"Did any of your friends get transferred here?" I asked.

"No, just me. Everyone else got to stay at Lacede. Lucky brats." Elena sighed, a soft, floaty sound. Even her sighs were beautiful. Mine came out sounding like a congested old man. "I wish I was back at Lacede now. I can't believe I have to spend the rest of high school *here*. Think I could convince my parents to move to the Lacede district?"

"Uh . . . I don't know," I said.

At the front of the room, a heavyset man with a shiny bald head called the class to order. "Welcome to the new school year," he said. "I'm Mr. Sale, and this is sophomore English, better known as world literature. As I call your name, please come forward to take one of these textbooks." He gestured toward a stack of thick books on the corner of his desk.

"As you all know, the school district lines were redrawn this summer and some former Lacede students were reassigned to Troy. We have one of those students in this class, Elena Argos," Mr. Sale continued.

Everyone turned to look at her and a few boys whistled. I would have sunk down in my seat if I had been singled out, but Elena just smiled back, dazzling everyone with her pearly whites and sparkling blue eyes.

"Let's make Elena and the other former Lacede students feel welcome here at Troy," Mr. Sale said. "I'm sure changing schools like this must be tough, and we should do everything we can to make this easier for them. Elena, welcome to Troy."

When the bell rang forty-five minutes later, Elena groaned loudly. "Can you believe Mr. Sale pointed me out like that?" she asked me as she stuffed her English book into her baby-pink backpack.

"Yeah," I said. "I'm sure everyone will be your best friend now that Mr. Sale told them to."

Elena laughed. "Exactly. That'll be *so* great for my reputation."

My stomach twisted just a little at her words. Elena needed to be concerned about more than Mr. Sale's pointing her out in class if she worried about her reputation. Talking to me wasn't the best plan.

"What class do you have next?" she asked as we walked into the hall.

I checked my schedule. "Algebra. You?"

"History." Elena made a face. "Oh, well, I guess maybe we'll see each other again later. I hope so, I need someone to talk to here or I'll go crazy."

I smiled. Life would go back to normal very soon, I knew. Once Elena got in with the In crowd at Troy, she'd forget all about me and I would go back to being ignored.

Only, I thought as I headed toward algebra, it had been really nice having someone to talk to before and after class. And having someone to roll my eyes with when Mr. Sale started talking about how this school year would help prepare us for the rest of our lives.

I enjoyed the thought of having a friend at Troy High. But she would dump me for the cool kids soon enough.

Later that day, I considered skipping lunch so I wouldn't have to be seen eating alone on the first day of school, but my stomach growled with hunger. I felt like I could eat about four bowls of watery school spaghetti, so after dropping my books off at my locker I made my way toward the cafeteria.

"Cassie, hey!" Elena appeared at my side as I walked through the double doors into the cafeteria. The Troy High cafeteria was actually really nice. Murals painted on the walls showed Trojan warriors riding to battle, their swords held high, with gods and goddesses watching from the clouds above them.

"Hey," I greeted her. "Are you getting lunch?"

Elena nodded. "I'm starving."

"Me too." We joined the hot lunch line and waited for our turn at the counter.

"Wow," Elena said, surveying the food. "It looks like the same old disgusting lunch they serve at Lacede. Do all the schools get their recipes from the same place?"

"Maybe they train their lunch ladies to cook the same way at every school in the country," I said, glancing at the lunch lady behind the counter, who spooned soupy mashed potatoes into Styrofoam bowls. "Like there's this team of teachers who go around the country showing them how to make Mystery Meat."

Elena laughed as she took a ham-and-cheese sandwich. "You're probably right."

I took the spaghetti and a bowl of peaches and a bowl of Jell-O and moved down the line toward the cash register. After Elena and I had gotten drinks and paid for our lunches, we turned to survey the cafeteria. Most of the tables were already taken, so I started to walk toward the door to the courtyard, where I usually ate outside alone.

"Come on, Cassie," Elena said. "I have a table for us already."

How had she gotten a table ahead of time? Could girls like Elena actually reserve tables in the school cafeteria?

I followed Elena as she wound through the tables toward the back of the room. In front of the mural showing Paris, the prince of Troy, giving the golden apple to the goddess Aphrodite, sat a table occupied by two cheerleaders, Kelsey and Mallory.

The girls turned to smile at Elena as she made her way toward them. When they spotted me, they exchanged confused glances. Elena didn't seem to notice.

"Hi, Elena," Kelsey said.

"Hey." Elena sat her tray down and gestured toward me. "Do you guys know Cassie?"

The girls smiled politely at me as I sat down at one of the empty seats.

"Hi," I said.

"Hey," Mallory said. I could see the name "Gassie" flashing through her mind.

I smiled, trying not to look as panicked as I felt. How had she done it? Elena had been at Troy for exactly half a day and already she'd made friends. Not just friends, but the Trojan equivalents of herself. I'd been going to school with these kids since kindergarten and they'd never let me into their group.

I was doomed. Once Elena realized I would never be

like her or Mallory or Kelsey, I'd be friendless at Troy once again.

I decided my best plan was to keep my mouth full so I couldn't talk and say something stupid in front of them. I began shoveling spaghetti into my mouth. I nearly gagged at the terrible taste, but I forced it down and kept chewing.

"Kelsey, Mallory, and I met last week at cheerleader orientation," Elena told me.

"So, how do you like Troy?" Mallory asked Elena, her eyes moving from Elena to me. She made a face before looking away.

"It's been great so far," Elena said. "Everyone is staring at me like I'm some kind of freak, but it's not too bad."

"You are a freak," Kelsey said, laughing. "A Spartan freak. But once the stench of Lacede wears off, you'll fit right in here."

"So how do you know Cassie?" Mallory asked.

My hands started to shake a little as I waited for Elena to tell them that we were just casual acquaintances, not real friends, and she'd only latched onto me that morning because she didn't want to be a friendless loser.

"Cassie and I have been best friends for years," Elena said. "Isn't that right, Cass?"

I stared at her, my hands frozen over my tray. Best friends? Years? Before today, I didn't think Elena even knew who I was other than her boyfriend's brother's friend.

"Uh," I said, trying to wrap my mind around the idea of being Elena Argos's best friend. "Yeah, best friends forever!"

Elena flashed me a wide smile and then bit into her sandwich.

The two girls looked from me to Elena and back again for a moment. Then they looked at each other, shrugged slightly, and resumed eating.

"Hello, ladies," said a drawling voice behind me. "How are the most beautiful girls at Troy today?"

I knew without turning around who the voice belonged to.

Kelsey giggled. "Hi, Perry," she said.

"And who is this?" Perry asked, his eyes locked on Elena.

I saw Mallory's eyebrows go up in surprise. "Haven't you already met your sister's best friend?" she asked.

Oh, nice. My voyage into popularity lasted all of, what? Five seconds?

But Elena seemed to be a quick thinker. "Cassie and I usually hang out at my house," Elena said. "Since I'm an only child and I have more privacy." She smiled at Perry and extended one hand. "Elena Argos. I used to go to Lacede."

"If I knew the Spartan girls were this gorgeous, I'd have changed schools a long time ago. I'm Perry Prince. I can't believe you've never introduced us before, dear little sister," he said, wrapping one arm around my neck in a hug and nearly strangling me. I slapped his arm away.

One glance at Elena told me she was just as smitten as Perry. Her cheeks had turned a faint pink color, making her look even prettier, which I didn't think could be possible. She glanced up at Perry, then looked away quickly, giggling.

I wanted to say something about Lucas, to remind Elena that she already had a boyfriend. But I also didn't want to lose the one possible friend at Troy I had.

"What grade are you in?" Perry asked Elena.

"I'm a sophomore," she told him.

"Oh, a young'un," Perry said, grinning. "I'm a junior."

I rolled my eyes. He talked as if he were a decade older than us. "You're just about ready for the retirement home, aren't you?" I asked.

No one seemed to hear my sarcasm. Or they ignored it if they did.

Perry glanced at his watch and then ran a hand through his hair. "I need to go. I've got some things to do before my next class. But it was great to meet you, Elena.

I'll definitely be seeing you around. If you ever need anything, find me."

Perry smiled one last time at Elena before he left.

Kelsey and Mallory leaned forward, squealing in unison.

"Perry is so crazy over you!" Mallory told Elena. "He is the hottest guy in school. Well, he and his brother, Hunter, who's a senior, are tied for hottest. But Perry is the hottest junior. And he'll definitely be asking you out sometime soon."

"Wait, wait," Kelsey said, waving her hands. "No one has asked Elena if she already has a boyfriend."

The two girls looked at her expectantly. I waited for Elena to tell them all about Lucas and how they'd been together off and on for years.

But Elena shook her head and said, "No, I don't have a boyfriend. No one at all."

3

"LEFT, RIGHT, LEFT, RIGHT, LEFT, RIGHT." MY band instructor, Ms. Holloway, clapped her hands as she chanted. The Troy High band marched across the edge of the football field, everyone trying to keep in step with one another. It was hot, the late summer sun beat down on our heads, and school had ended nearly an hour ago.

But Ms. Holloway devoted her life to band practice and she said we didn't have time to waste, with homecoming only two months away.

We weren't the only ones suffering in the sun. The football players were throwing balls and running into tackling dummies in preparation for the game that weekend. The cheerleaders had been practicing cheers and pyramids, but were now lying on the grass, working on their tans and watching the football team.

"Left, Cassie," Ms. Holloway said. "Left, right, *left*, right."

Oh, give it up, Ms. Holloway. I could never keep in step last year, why did she think this year would be any different?

We were forced to endure another fifteen minutes of marching in circles while trying to play the Troy High school song before Ms. Holloway finally let us go. Sweat had soaked my back and my hair clung to my neck.

"Hey, Cassie," Elena greeted me as she made her way over to where I'd left my backpack and flute case. Mallory and Kelsey followed her. "How was your practice?"

"Torture," I said. "I need a cold shower."

Mallory made a face. "I'm glad I dumped band for cheerleading," she said. "One year of marching in the sun was more than enough."

And yet, *jumping* around in the sun was somehow better? It didn't make sense to me, but I figured it must be popular-girl logic.

"You should join cheerleading," Elena told me. "Then we could hang out together at practice."

I snorted. "Me? A cheerleader? Did you not see me unable to keep in step while marching? I'm way too uncoordinated to even think about cheerleading."

Elena pouted. "Oh, well, I guess we can still hang out after practice and whenever we get a break at the games." She bounced on the balls of her feet. "I can't wait until the game on Saturday! It'll be so much fun."

"I'm just looking forward to seeing the guys in those tight football pants," Kelsey said, grinning as her gaze roamed over the football field.

"Well, yeah, that's a given!" Elena said, giggling.

"Especially one guy in particular," Mallory said, nudging Elena's side. "Right?"

Elena's cheeks reddened. "Maybe."

Coach Wellens blew his whistle to signal the end of the practice, and the football players headed off the field. It was easy to pick out Hunter from the other guys. He stood taller than most, with broad shoulders and a thick, muscled body. Perry was tall too, though not as tall as Hunter, and thinner, with lean muscle and a narrow frame. They even walked off the field differently: Hunter kind of stomped, his body still rigid and tense from practice, while Perry casually sauntered off the field, as if the workout had no effect on him at all.

"Hello, ladies," Perry said when he reached our little circle. He threw an arm around Elena's shoulders and grinned down at her. "How's it going?"

"Ew," Elena said, wrinkling her nose. "You smell sweaty."

She didn't make any movement to get away from his stench.

"My apologies, dear lady," Perry said, making a mocking, sweeping bow. "I shall now head to the showers to wash away the stench of my manly toil."

I rolled my eyes.

But obviously I was the only one who thought Perry's display was revolting. Elena, Mallory, and Kelsey all giggled and waved to him as he joined the line of guys headed toward the little gray building that housed the locker rooms.

Mallory and Kelsey let out an earsplitting squeal.

"Did you see the way he put his arm around you?" Kelsey asked Elena.

"He totally wants to go out with you," Mallory said.

"Don't you think so, Cassie?" Kelsey asked me. "I mean, you're Perry's sister. You know him better than we do."

I knew my brother liked to flirt with pretty girls. And I knew Elena was just his type.

I also knew from the bad feeling in my stomach that things were not going to end well now that Elena Argos had come to Troy. Especially not if she let her fascination with my brother make her forget about her longtime boyfriend.

All three girls were looking at me as if waiting for an answer, so I said, "Um, yeah, I guess so."

Elena slipped her arm through mine. "Tell me all about him," she said. "What's he like? What does he like to do for fun?"

I could tell her how Perry always managed to weasel his way out of doing his chores. Or about how when we were kids he tore the arms off my favorite doll. Or even about how he fell madly in love with girls for two weeks and then got tired of them and moved on to someone else.

But I knew Elena didn't want to hear any of that. And if I didn't watch myself, I'd end up sitting alone in the cafeteria again. I'd have to walk home from band practice by myself instead of standing with the three prettiest girls at Troy High, gossiping about boys.

And there was something about Elena. Things were different when I was around her. I wanted to be like her. She made me want to be pretty and popular and crazy over football players (although not football players who happened to be my brothers, because that would be gross).

I wanted Elena to be my friend. And I was afraid that the only way to have that was to tell her what she wanted to hear.

"Perry is such a great big brother," I gushed. "He's really funny and always helps out around the house. He's a really great guy. He loves action movies and football, of course, and he sometimes helps my dad work on the family car. Perry is really smart about mechanical stuff."

Elena squeezed my arm. "He's not seeing anyone, is he? Or is there anyone he likes?"

"No, I don't think so," I said. "Well, obviously he must like you, with the way he's been acting since he met you at lunch. But I haven't heard him say anything about liking anyone else."

Elena stopped walking and turned toward me. Kelsey and Mallory stood behind her, with matching grins as they watched Elena.

"Cassie, can you do me a huge favor?" Elena asked. "Tonight at home, can you somehow find out what Perry really thinks of me? Find out if he truly likes me? I'll give you my cell number and you can call me right away. I have to know every detail about what he says and how he says it. Okay?" Her blue eyes sparkled as she looked at me, her smile hopeful. I felt as if she were entrusting me with an important task. And no one else could do this for her.

I nodded. "Sure," I promised.

◆ ◆ ◆

"How was the first day of school?" Mom asked over dinner that night.

Family dinners consisted of the five of us eating in various places around the living room while watching TV.

I sat on the floor, with my plate on the coffee table. "Fine," I answered.

"Not bad," Perry said, shrugging.

"Uh-huh," Hunter grunted, his eyes glued to the TV.

"Sounds like a great day," Dad said, smirking. "How was football practice, guys?"

"Good," Hunter said. "Coach said my throwing arm is looking great."

Dad nodded approvingly. "I knew all that practice this summer would improve your arm," he said. "Not that it needed much improving." He grinned.

"So, Cassie," Mom said, "how were your classes?"

Mom always asked that. And I knew that what she always really wanted to ask was, "Did you make any friends today?" It practically killed my mom that I wasn't as popular as she had been in school. My dad had been a football player and my mom a cheerleader. They were like the perfect, popular couple. They'd had two perfect, popular kids. And then they'd had me.

I'd spent my entire life convinced that I must have been adopted.

"My classes were fine," I said, stirring a cucumber around in a puddle of salad dressing on my plate. "I have a friend in my English class."

Mom's face lit up so much you'd think I had just told

her Santa Claus was coming down the chimney right at that moment. "You do? Who is it?"

"Elena Argos," I said. "She's one of the kids who got transferred to Troy from Lacede for the redistricting. We have a couple of classes together. And we knew each other already because she—"

I caught myself just in time. I almost said that we knew each other because she was dating Greg's brother. I had a feeling that spilling the beans about Elena's relationship status in front of Perry probably wasn't the way to win her friendship.

But why shouldn't I say something? Elena *was* dating Lucas. Perry had a right to know that before he had any serious thoughts about dating her.

And yet, I couldn't bring myself to say anything.

Maybe Elena and Lucas really weren't together anymore, I told myself. They could have broken up last night after I left Greg's house. Elena and Lucas breaking up was nothing new. Every few months, they had a huge fight and swore they'd never speak to each other ever again. Then three weeks later, they were back together, proclaiming how they were soul mates.

But wouldn't Elena have been upset today if they had broken up? Or maybe she had become so used to it that it didn't even bother her anymore?

I had to keep my mouth shut for a little while.

"How do you know Elena?" Mom asked me.

"Oh," I said, trying to think quickly, "we met at the community pool last year." I shoved a forkful of salad into my mouth and focused on chewing.

"I can't believe Elena is a sophomore," Perry said through a mouthful of steak. "She seems so much more sophisticated. Sophomores are babies."

I rolled my eyes.

"You were a sophomore just last year," Hunter reminded him.

Perry waved a hand. "Exactly my point. Last year, I was just a kid. This year, I'm much more mature." He let out a loud burp. "Excuse me. See? Last year I wouldn't have said excuse me after burping. This year I have manners."

Oh, puh-lease. When had he suddenly developed these manners? Right after he had held me down and farted on me two days ago?

"But there's something different about Elena," Perry said. The corners of his mouth curled into a slight smile. "She's not like the other girls at school. Not like anyone I've ever met."

"You've only talked to her twice," I pointed out.

"But I can tell," Perry insisted. "She's special, I can feel it." He put his plate down on his knee and looked at me. "Cassie, you have to help me get her."

I swallowed the food in my mouth. "Get her what?"

"You know, get her to go out with me. I haven't been able to stop thinking about her all day. Do you know if she's seeing anyone?"

This was it. This was the time to tell my brother the truth. Maybe I could find a way to break it to him gently.

But the way Perry looked at me made me remember the way Elena had looked that afternoon. Perry and Elena could become the most popular couple at Troy High. And if I kept my mouth shut and went along for the ride, I could be popular too.

I didn't owe any loyalty to Lucas anyway. What had he ever done for me?

I tried to push thoughts of Greg out of mind as I said, "I don't think she's seeing anyone right now."

Perry smiled wide at me. "Great. Tomorrow I'll work my magic on Elena Argos."

4

"BUT WHAT SHOULD I DO?" ELENA ASKED ON the phone later that evening.

I lay on my back across my bed, staring up at the ceiling. I couldn't believe Elena Argos was asking *me* for advice. "I don't know."

"Lucas and I have been together a long time," Elena said. "But we keep breaking up. It's not a healthy relationship, is it?"

"You guys have broken up fifty times in the last year. I think you should be experts at it by now."

"But those breakups were different," Elena explained. "We always knew they weren't forever, but this time it is. Once I tell Lucas it's over, it's *really* over. I want to do this right. I don't want to make him go crazy or anything."

"That's . . . considerate, I guess."

"I still care about him, but I'm not in love with him anymore."

"Then you shouldn't be with a guy who you don't like in that way."

Elena sighed. "I wish this were easier. But I think I really like Perry. I can't stop thinking about him. And I can't believe he actually likes *me*."

"He does," I said. "He said he's been thinking about you all day."

I had to hold the phone away from my ear to keep from going deaf at Elena's squeal.

"A little warning next time, please," I grumbled.

"Oh, Cassie, you don't know how happy you've made me," Elena said. "I could come over there right now and kiss you."

"Better not, my kissing seems to scare people away."

Elena didn't seem to hear my comment. Or she didn't care, as I could hear her rustling through something on the other end of the line.

"What are you doing?" I asked.

"Trying to pick out the perfect outfit for tomorrow," she said. "I want to look my best when I see Perry at school."

I thought Elena always looked her best regardless.

"Okay, then," I said. "I'll let you go. I need to do my homework anyway."

"Okay. Thanks for everything, Cassie. You're a great fake best friend," Elena joked, laughing.

I laughed. "That's my job."

As I hung up the phone, I thought about Greg. What was I doing helping Perry and Elena get together? How mad would Greg be if he found out I'd had a part in breaking his brother's heart?

I found myself picking up the phone again and dialing his number.

"Hello?"

My stomach jumped. Lucas had answered the phone. Could he sense I had just talked to his girlfriend and knew she planned to break up with him?

"H-hi, Lucas," I said, trying to sound normal even though my voice trembled a little. "Is Greg home?"

"Hold on," Lucas said.

A moment later, Greg picked up the phone. "Hey, Cassie," he said. His voice sounded a little weird, lower than normal.

"Hey," I said.

There was silence as I tried to think of something to say. Memories of our kiss flooded into my head.

I took a deep breath, trying to steady myself. "Look,

Greg, let's just forget about . . . you know. Okay? It was a mistake."

Greg was silent a moment, then said, "Okay. Forgotten."

He didn't like the kiss. That was obvious. I was so incredibly stupid. Why hadn't someone invented a time machine so I could go back and undo the biggest mistake of my life?

"So," I said, pushing away those thoughts, "why haven't you called me today? You always call after the first day of school to see how things went."

"Sorry," Greg said. "I had this student council meeting after school and now I'm working on ideas for fund-raisers we can have this year. I didn't realize being the tenth-grade class president would be so much work. It's a good thing I decided not to try doing this and band at the same time."

Greg had quit band after his freshman year when he was voted class president for the upcoming year. I was a bit disappointed, since band had brought Greg and me together in the first place.

"You were the one who wanted to be president," I reminded him. "You could have stayed with us band geeks and just showed up at games when needed."

Greg laughed. "I know, but student council will give me more experience than band would if I hope to get into politics one day. Besides, I kind of like being in charge.

The other class officers kept looking to me for ideas and approval during our meeting today."

"A nice stroke to your ego, I'm sure," I said, rolling my eyes as I settled back into the pillows on my bed.

"And it gets me out of Lucas's shadow," Greg said. "I'm sure you know how that feels."

Of course I did. I'd done nothing but live in Hunter's and Perry's shadows my entire life.

"So how did your first day of school go?" Greg asked.

I rolled onto my side and ran a fingernail over a loose thread on my comforter. "Fine," I said. "The same old thing, I guess."

I couldn't tell Greg about Elena and Perry. Part of me wanted to and knew I should, but the other part really didn't want to mess up this budding friendship with Elena. It felt nice having someone notice that I was around. I loved having Greg as my best friend, but I also liked having a girl to talk to. Maybe I could even eventually talk to Elena about Greg. She had more experience with guys than I did, so maybe she could tell me what to do about the feelings I had for him.

"There weren't any riots in the halls because of the former Spartans now attending Troy?"

I laughed. "No, everything seemed to go fine. An uneasy alliance, I guess, since we're all forced together."

"Did you see Elena?"

I swallowed hard, trying to keep from sounding as panicked as I felt at his question. Why was he asking me about Elena? Did he suspect something?

"Yeah, we have English together," I told him. "And we have the same lunch period. Oh, and the cheerleaders were outside practicing at the same time the band was, so. I saw her then too."

"The Spartan cheerleaders aren't going to be too happy to hear that she's now cheering for the Trojans," Greg said.

"Well, she can't help that her house is now inside the Troy district," I pointed out.

"I know, but this rivalry makes people crazy. Lucas is already making comments that the Lacede students now attending Troy should have all convinced their parents to move into the Lacede district so they wouldn't have to change schools."

There was definitely no way I could tell Greg that I knew Elena planned to break up with Lucas. If Lucas already felt this hostile about something that people had no control over, how would he react to the news?

Greg sighed. "I should go. I have a ton of stuff to read over from last year's sophomore president."

"Okay," I said.

"Hey," Greg said, "want to come hang out with me at Lacede's game on Friday night?"

My heart sped up a little at the thought of spending Friday night with Greg. "Sure," I said.

"Great. See you then. Good night, Cassie."

5

"HEY," ELENA SAID WHEN SHE FOUND ME AT my locker after school the next afternoon. "We're all going to the Ice Cream Factory. Come on."

I looked over her shoulder and saw Mallory and Kelsey waiting nearby. "Me?" I asked. I had never been asked to go to the Ice Cream Factory with anyone.

"Yes, you," Elena said, laughing and tossing back her blond waves. "We're all going. Don't keep us waiting."

"Who's we?" I asked as I shut my locker and let Elena lead me down the hall toward Mallory and Kelsey.

"Come on, Cassie," Mallory said, sneering. "Don't be such a slowpoke."

The girls led me outside to the parking lot, past the losers' circle, where the geeks and loners watched us as we laughed and talked on our way outside. In the parking lot, three cars waited along the edge of the grass.

My brothers' Toyota sat at the front of the line, with Hunter in the driver's seat and Perry next to him. Behind them was a car filled with football players and another filled with cheerleaders.

"Come on!" Perry called, waving to us.

I hung back a bit, expecting my brothers to say something about my tagging along when they got sight of me. But Perry jumped out of the car and opened the back door, smiling.

Elena, Mallory, and I climbed into the backseat of my brothers' car while Kelsey got into the car with the cheerleaders. I sat in the middle, with Mallory on one side and Elena on the other. Perry turned the stereo up loud, so that the bass vibrated through the car and up my body. Mallory and Elena bounced around, dancing in their seats. Perry drummed on the dashboard. Hunter tapped his fingers on the steering wheel.

I was hanging out with the popular crowd. I started imitating Mallory's and Elena's movements, trying to get into the groove of the music. So this was what it was like to be popular. It wasn't so hard. It was actually pretty fun.

The car skidded to a stop in front of the Ice Cream Factory and we climbed out. Our group took up four booths along the wall of the small shop. We were loud and rude, shouting out orders and making jokes. Some of the guys tossed a football across the booths and no one even asked them to stop. It seemed that the football players and cheerleaders could do whatever they wanted.

And I was right there in the middle of it all, seated next to Elena. Perry had seated himself across from Elena, and he kept leaning over the table to touch her arm or tug on a lock of her blond hair. And whenever Perry would look away to talk to one of his friends, Elena would turn to me and give me that excited look that I'd seen girls exchange whenever the guy they liked paid attention to them. Elena could have given that look to Mallory or Kelsey, but instead she looked at me.

"Hey, Cassie," Perry said while we were all eating our sundaes. "The band is ready to play the victory march tomorrow, right?"

The guys all roared enthusiastically. I stared at my brother, shocked that he knew the band even played at games. I'd never seen him glance in the band's direction.

"Yeah," I said. "We're ready."

"And so are the cheerleaders," Elena said.

"Because we have a secret weapon," Mallory said, grinning at Elena. "Lacede's best cheerleader is now Troy's!"

Elena blushed. "Well, I don't know about *best*."

"Oh, stop being so modest," Kelsey told her. "You're amazing and you know it."

Elena's cheeks turned even redder. "Thanks. I hope I live up to all this."

"Hey, Cassie, come help me outside for a minute," Perry said. I followed him reluctantly.

"What do you want?" I asked once we were outside.

Perry turned to me, his eyes wide and wild. "I need you to give something to Elena for me."

I rolled my eyes. "Oh, come on. You were sitting right there across the table from her thirty seconds ago. Couldn't you have given it to her then?"

"I don't want to do it in front of everyone," Perry said. "Please, Cassie, you have to help me. I really like her, but I don't want to mess things up. Just read this note and tell me if I'm being too forward."

He held out a hand, a piece of paper pinched between his fingers. I stared at it, my nose wrinkling. The pink paper had flowers on the edges.

"You have got to be kidding me," I muttered.

"Please," he said again.

"I'm not your personal messenger!" But I took the note and unfolded it, reading over the words as quickly as I could.

Elena,

I can't stop thinking about you. Last night I dreamed we kissed, and I'm dying to make that a reality. Meet me outside, under the big oak tree?

Perry

"What do you think?" Perry asked in a low voice.

"I think I'm going to be sick," I said honestly. "What happened to, 'Do you like me? Check yes or no.'"

"This isn't third grade," Perry said. "I have to be suave."

I waved the pink floral-print note at him. "And having your sister deliver your love letters makes you suave?"

Perry turned me around and pushed me toward the doors. "Just go give it to her."

I walked back inside, clenching the note in my fist. Was this what love did to a person? Made them write stupid love letters and force their sisters into doing their dirty work?

But why was I surprised? I already knew love made people do stupid things—like kissing their best friends and almost ruining a perfectly good friendship.

I sat down in my seat and pressed the note into Elena's hand. "Here," I said. "I was told to give this to you."

Elena gave me a puzzled look, but when she read

the note her expression changed completely. Her cheeks turned pink and a smile spread across her face.

"Be right back," she whispered to me, giggling.

When Elena and Perry returned a few minutes later, Elena grabbed my hand and said, "We have to go to the bathroom *now*."

I had a spoonful of ice cream in my hand when she grabbed it and so it splattered onto the table. I looked back sadly at my melting sundae as Elena dragged me toward the women's room.

When we were inside, Elena checked the stalls to make sure we were alone, then she turned to me, her eyes wide.

"What happened?" I asked.

"Oh, Cassie, I can't believe it," she said quickly in one breath. She grabbed my hands, squeezing tight. "He likes me. Perry actually likes me!"

I pulled my hands out of her death grip and grimaced. "Well, yeah," I said. "That's obvious."

"I couldn't believe it until I heard it for myself." Elena leaned back against a sink, hugging her arms to her chest. "He said he's never met anyone as beautiful as I am and he can't stop thinking about me. He's just so . . . *amazing*. I can't believe he would choose *me*."

Amazing? My brother? Not a word I would ever use to describe him.

"Why wouldn't he choose you?" I asked. "You *are* beautiful, and everyone at Troy loves you already."

Elena blushed, shaking her head. "Thank you for everything, Cassie. You've been a great friend. I worried I'd be all alone here at Troy, but you've helped me fit in so well. I can't thank you enough."

I hadn't done anything to help Elena gain status at Troy, but if she felt thankful toward me, I wasn't about to stomp on it.

"So," I said, watching her as she practically danced around the bathroom, "does this mean you and Lucas have broken up?"

Elena blinked at me, her smile faltering a bit. "What?"

"You know, Lucas? The guy who's been your boyfriend for the last three years."

"Oh." Elena waved a hand, as if this wasn't important. "We haven't broken up *yet*, but we will."

My eyebrows shot upward. "You haven't broken up with Lucas? But I thought you were so crazy over Perry?"

"I am," Elena said. "I'm going to break up with Lucas before I go out with Perry. I promise. Don't worry, Cassie, I'll treat your brother right."

It wasn't *my* brother I was worried about.

6

"YOU LOOK RIDICULOUS," I SAID.

Greg turned to look at me, rubbing at the blue face paint on his cheeks.

"I feel ridiculous," he said. "But everyone is wearing face paint to show their support and as class president, I can't be the only nonpainted face in the crowd."

I looked around at the sea of blue-and-white faces in the bleachers. "You know, at Troy we just yell and wear Troy High T-shirts."

Greg grinned. "At Lacede, we like to go all-out."

"The game is about to start," I said. "Do you think I should sit here or the visitors' side?"

I noticed the looks I got from a few Spartans and their supporters. Maybe it would be safer to try to blend in with the Southern Mills supporters on the other side of the field.

"Sit here," Greg said. "No one will mess with you, if you can deal with the glares."

"Okay," I said. We found seats halfway up the bleachers, near a group of girls who gave me dark scowls.

"We've got the spirit! We can succeed! We've got the moves! Go, go Lacede!" The Lacede cheerleaders leaped into the air, waving their pom-poms and shrieking at the top of their lungs as they urged the crowd on.

The teams emerged from the locker rooms to loud cheers. Lucas and the Southern Mills team captain met on the fifty-yard line and shook hands before heading to their respective sides of the field.

I wasn't a huge fan of football, but the game stayed tense enough to keep my interest. The crowd around me roared whenever the Spartans scored or booed whenever the Southern Mills Wildcats did.

At halftime, the teams were tied 14–14.

All around me, people stood up to head down to the refreshment stands.

"Want to share a hot dog?" Greg asked.

"Okay," I agreed. "But no onions on my half."

"Don't blame me if the onions spill over to your side."

We joined the long line for the hot dogs. After several minutes, the line hadn't moved much.

"I'm starving," Greg said. "This line is moving too slow. Got anything to eat?"

I shook my head. "I had a mint left, but I ate it during the first quarter."

But Greg didn't seem to hear what I said. He was focused on something in the direction of the locker rooms. I turned to see what he was looking at.

Elena and Lucas stood outside the gray building. From the way their arms moved as they spoke, it didn't look as though she were wishing him good luck.

She wouldn't dare. Not here. Not *now*.

Would she?

"Um, Greg," I said, trying to sound nonchalant, "how have Lucas and Elena been doing lately?"

"Not so great, from the looks of it," Greg said, his eyes still on them. "Come on, let's see what's going on."

We left the hot-dog line and hurried across the grass toward the locker rooms. When we'd drawn closer, I could hear Elena speaking.

"You never pay attention to me anymore! It's always football or video games or your stupid friends."

"I spent all of Saturday with you last weekend!" Lucas shouted. His face had turned red and the veins in his neck bulged behind his shoulder padding. "I followed you around the mall for four hours while you looked at fifty different pairs of shoes and didn't buy a single thing! What more do you want?"

Elena crossed her arms over her chest. "Nothing, Lucas. That's just it. I don't want anything else from you ever again."

"Hey," Greg said, stepping between them. "Everything okay?"

"Yes," Lucas said at the same time Elena said "No."

Lucas stared at her. "So that's it? You want to throw away three years of us?"

"We haven't been together three years, we've spent at least half of that time broken up!" Elena exclaimed. "We were never meant to be together, I see that now. That's why we've never been able to make this work more than a few months at a time."

"Whoa," Greg said, holding his hands up. "I think maybe you guys need to take some time to calm down and think this over. Wait until tomorrow, when you can talk about this rationally."

"I've already thought this over," Elena said. "And breaking up for good is the right solution. Lucas, once you get over being angry at me, you'll see that this is right for both of us."

She had to do this *now*, when Lucas had to put his focus on the game?

"Elena," I said, "I think Greg is right. Don't make any decisions now that you'll regret tomorrow. Wait until you both can sit down in private and talk. Lucas has other things on his mind right now—"

"I'm not making any decisions I'll regret. I've made up my mind, and it's final."

At that moment, Perry appeared around the side of the building and said, "Hey, Elena, ready to go?" He shot her a grin, oblivious to the tension in the air.

My pulse pounded in my ears. I could barely hear anything over the sound.

Lucas's and Greg's bodies tensed as they both gazed back at Perry.

"What do you want with Elena?" Lucas asked in a deep voice.

"None of your business, Spartan," Perry snapped.

Lucas took a step forward. The muscles in his arms were rigid and his fists were clenched at his sides. "Anything involving my girlfriend is my business."

"I'm not your girlfriend anymore, Lucas!" Elena exclaimed.

Lucas grabbed Elena's arm. "Elena, listen—"

Perry stepped forward. "Let her go."

"And what are you going to do about it, pretty boy?" Lucas asked.

If I were Perry, I would have thought twice about standing up to Lucas. Lucas had several inches and pounds on my brother.

Suddenly the Spartan locker-room door swung open and Coach Whittingham stuck his head out. "Mennon! What are you doing out here? The second half is about to start, and we're waiting on you so we can talk strategy."

Lucas looked at him, blinking, as if he'd forgotten where he was. He looked down at his uniform, then back at the coach and nodded as he stomped into the locker room. He shot a dark glare back at Elena and Perry.

"You coming with us, Cassie?" Elena asked, sounding just as perky and happy as usual, as if the last five minutes hadn't happened.

Behind us, people were returning to their seats, waiting for the game to resume. In the distance, I could hear the rumble of hundreds of voices talking all at once. But in our little corner, everything was silent, as if waiting for me to make a decision. Who to go with—my old friend or new one?

Greg turned away from us and said in a cold voice, "I have to get back."

He ambled away without saying anything else.

"Let's get out of here," Perry said. "I can't stand to be around so many Spartans much longer."

Elena held a hand out to me, smiling. I let her take my hand and lead me toward the gate behind Perry.

7

"CASSIE," MOM CALLED FROM BEHIND MY CLOSED door. "Cassie, wake up. You have a visitor."

I rolled over, grumbling into my pillow. It was too early. I had stayed up half the night wondering if I had done the right thing by keeping my mouth shut about Elena and Perry. I felt like no matter what choice I made, I would have hurt someone I cared about.

I heard the door open. "Cassie, get up. It's almost noon and you have a guest."

Moaning, I lifted my head from my pillow and opened one eye to look at Mom. "Who is it?" I asked.

The door opened wider and I saw Elena standing in the hall, looking unbelievably gorgeous at this time of day. I sat up, trying to shift my Tweety Bird pajamas into position and reaching up to smooth down my rat's nest of hair.

"I think she's awake now, Elena," Mom said. She shot an amused smile my way, raising her eyebrows, and then disappeared down the hall.

Elena bounced into my room and sat on the edge of my bed. "Morning, sleepyhead!"

I winced at the sound of her voice. "Not so loud. I just woke up."

"You're sleeping the whole day away," Elena told me, laughing. "It's time to wake up. Perry isn't here. He and Hunter are doing some pregame tradition thing." She got up and walked over to my dresser, picking up necklaces and CDs at random to inspect them.

"Waffles," I said. Hunter and Perry always met the other guys from the football team for breakfast on game day, a longstanding Trojan tradition.

"Yeah," Elena said. "I was up and decided to come by and see you. And tell you about what an amazing night Perry and I had after we left the football game."

Perry had dropped Hunter and me off at home around ten, and then he and Elena took the car back out to drive around for a while.

"It was so incredible, Cassie," Elena said, leaning against my dresser to sigh at her reflection in the mirror. Dozens of pictures of Greg and me that I had taped along the sides of the mirror framed her face: "We went to the park and it was all lit up by the streetlights. We were alone and Perry pushed me on the swings for a while. Then we lay in the grass and looked at the stars. It was so romantic. And the way he kisses! I haven't kissed anyone like that ever. Lucas was always such a sloppy kisser, but Perry is amazing."

I shifted in my seat. "I don't really want to hear all the gory details."

"I know breaking up with Lucas was the right thing to do," Elena told me. "I knew it before, but I'm *completely* sure now. Perry is the guy I'm meant to be with. It was fate for me to be transferred to Troy."

"Elena," I said, "did you happen to think that maybe you shouldn't have broken up with Lucas last night?"

Elena looked at me as if I were the crazy one. "It wouldn't have been fair to keep dating Lucas when I'm in love with Perry."

"No, it wouldn't," I agreed. "But you could have chosen a different time to dump Lucas. He really needed to focus on the game and not on you."

To her credit, Elena did look sorry as she twisted one of my beaded bracelets in her hands. "I thought it would be better this way, if he could use the game to work out his anger."

I sighed. "I don't think your plan worked."

"Lucas kept calling my cell last night," Elena said. "And he's already started this morning. He's left about twenty messages, begging me to go back to him."

"Maybe he really loves you," I said.

"Then he should have taken the time to show it before now," Elena said. She pulled her cell out of her pocket and punched a few buttons. "Here, listen to this."

She pressed the phone to my ear and I heard Lucas's voice. He sounded weird, his voice higher than usual, with a desperate pitch to it. "Elena, *please*," he said. "What does that Trojan jerk have that I don't? We've been together for years. You know I love you. I'll do anything to get you back. I'll be a better boyfriend, I promise—"

I felt uncomfortable listening to Lucas pour his heart out to Elena's voice mail, and I pushed the phone away. "Are you sure breaking up with Lucas is what you really want?" I asked. "He doesn't seem so bad, as far as jocks go."

"The way I feel about Perry, it's . . . different. Amazing. I've never felt this way about anyone before." She gave me a half-smile. "I made the right decision, I'm sure. And now I'll let you go back to sleep." She stood and started toward my door. "By the way," she said, pausing to point to one of the pictures taped to my mirror, "I can't believe Greg let you put that horrible picture up."

The picture was from band camp two years ago, when Greg and I had first met. He had thick braces, bad acne, and hair that he had tried to grow out that year to look cool but instead looked like a huge frizzball. I had taken the picture on our last day at camp, when I had dared Greg to stuff as many grapes into his mouth as he could during breakfast. His cheeks puffed out like a chipmunk's full of nuts, and he grinned wide, showing the mouthful of grapes and braces, which had remnants of his breakfast stuck in them.

It was one of my favorite pictures ever and it always made me happy to look at it.

I thought about Greg and the anger I'd seen in his eyes the night before. "Is Perry really worth all the trouble you caused?" I asked.

Elena turned back to me, her eyes shining. "Of course!"

I tried to smile as she waved and left the room.

◆ ◆ ◆

I was thankful that Greg didn't suspect that I'd known Elena planned to dump Lucas for Perry. At least no one had given that secret away during the scene the night before.

But I still worried a little that Greg might be mad at me for leaving the game to go with Elena and Perry, so I called him and got him to agree to meet me at TJ's, our favorite pizza place on Lacede's side of town. We always ordered the same thing, a large thin-crust pizza with everything, no mushrooms on Greg's half and extra mushrooms on mine.

He walked into the restaurant five minutes later. Glancing quickly at me, he moved toward the table, his hands buried deep in his pockets and his eyes focused on the floor.

"Hey," he said as he slid into the seat across from me.

"Hi," I answered.

We were silent for nearly a full minute. I played with the paper from my straw wrapper while I tried to think of the right thing to say.

Millie, our waitress, saved me from having to decide right away. "Hey, honey," she greeted Greg. We were at TJ's so often that she knew our names, but she always called everyone honey. "The usual?"

Greg nodded.

"Okay," Millie said, smiling wide. "I'll be right back with your Coke and the pizza."

Once again, we were alone, sitting silently. Greg stared at the wall over my shoulder.

"Hi, Greg!" some girls called as they walked into the restaurant. Spartan cheerleaders. I recognized them from the game. I shot a quick glare at their backs as they headed across the room.

The jealousy that flooded through me helped give me courage.

"I'm really sorry," I said. "I shouldn't have left the game with Elena after what happened."

"You didn't have to stay," Greg said. "But I kind of thought that you might. I thought we were best friends."

"We are," I said softly. "But I wasn't sure that you wanted to see me right then, since you walked away like that. And Elena had just dumped your brother for mine."

Millie returned with Greg's drink and the pizza. Once she had left and we had both served ourselves a slice, Greg said, "Why would that make me not want to see you?"

I twisted a string of cheese around my finger. "I don't know. It just seemed like you might be mad at me."

"No, I'm mad at Elena and Perry. Lucas is my brother, so I have to be mad at them."

"And Perry is my brother," I pointed out. "But that doesn't mean I have any hard feelings toward Lucas." I put my pizza down on my plate and looked at him. "How's he doing, anyway?"

"He's doing as well as he can after being dumped," Greg said. "He messed up a lot of easy plays last night during the second half. We lost, by the way, 38–14. Coach called the house last night after the game, and he and Lucas talked for a long time. Lucas isn't punching holes in the wall, so I assume that's a good sign."

I sighed. "Good. I told Elena this morning that she should have chosen a different time to break up with him."

"You talked to Elena this morning?"

I looked at the clock on the wall. "Well, actually it was only about an hour ago. I slept really late today. She came over to tell me—" I broke off, realizing what I was about to say.

"To tell you what?" Greg asked.

I stared down at the table, tracing a crack in the laminate with my fingernail. "To tell me about her night with Perry."

Greg gripped his glass in one hand, his knuckles tight. "That girl is . . . Ugh, I can't even think of an adequate word to describe her. She stomps all over Lucas's heart and then she just goes off with her new boyfriend."

"I know," I said. "She does feel bad, though. She thought it would be good for Lucas to work out his frustrations during the game."

Greg sat in silence, stirring his Coke with his straw. I chewed my pizza, watching him.

"So what's going on with you and Elena?" he asked.

I shrugged. "We're friends."

"Elena Argos has never given you a second look during all the times she's seen you at my house, and now she's suddenly your new best friend?"

I raised one eyebrow at him. "She's not my *best* friend."

Greg's ears reddened a bit. "You can be friends with whoever you want. I just thought the two of you were an odd pairing, that's all."

"Why?" I snapped. "Because Elena is so beautiful and popular and I'm just some plain, unnoticeable dork?"

"You know I don't think that," Greg said, staring hard at me. "But really, what do you and Elena have in common?"

I sat up straighter. "Lots of stuff," I said. "Girl stuff that *you* would never understand."

Greg rolled his eyes. Before he could speak, the chime on the door sounded and Lucas walked in, followed by his friends Owen, Ackley, and Patrick. I knew Owen better than Ackley or Patrick, although all of them were on Lacede's football team and I'd seen them around Greg and Lucas's house several times. Owen was friendly, but Ackley kept more to himself and was always shadowed by his best friend, Patrick. Also, I doubted Ackley had wanted to spend much time in my presence over the past year, ever since Hunter injured his ankle in the game between Lacede and Troy.

Lucas headed in our direction when he spotted Greg and me.

"Well, if it isn't a Trojan in Spartan territory," Lucas said, looking down at me. He looked tired, with dark circles under his eyes.

"Leave her alone, Lucas," Greg told him.

Lucas, ignoring his brother, leaned down so that he was eye level with me. "Tell your brother that he has no idea what he's started. Steal from me, and you have to deal with every Spartan wanting revenge."

"Cassie has nothing to do with what her brother does," Greg said.

Lucas turned toward Greg. "You, little brother, need to decide who you're loyal to. What's it going to be? Family or friend?"

My heart felt as if it were running a marathon inside my chest. I had never seen that wild look in Lucas's eyes before. I didn't doubt for a moment that he could and would do something to have revenge.

"Don't do anything stupid, Lucas," Greg said in a calm voice. "You're just really upset right now. Take a few days to settle down."

"He won't listen," Owen spoke up, shaking his head. "I've already tried. He just says that I owe him allegiance if I want to keep my position on the football team and, well,

I'm really counting on a football scholarship for college." He shrugged and shot me an apologetic look.

"The Trojans will pay," Patrick said, punching a fist into one hand. "I can't wait to get my hands on them."

"Especially that big Trojan quarterback," Ackley growled, glaring at me. "I owe him payback for what he did to me last year."

"No one takes anything from me and gets away with it," Lucas said. "Perry Prince has started a war."

8

THAT NIGHT, I RODE TO TROY WITH MY PARENTS.
Perry and Hunter had already left an hour before to get
ready for the game. I wore my band uniform, with my
red plumed helmet tucked under one arm and my flute
case in the other.

"Isn't this exciting?" Mom asked, her eyes shining
as she looked around at the number of people milling
between the gate and the bleachers. "Everyone around
here really comes out to support the football team."

"We take pride in our boys," Dad said, puffing his
chest out. I could already tell he was reminiscing about
his own football days. I had to make my escape before
he started in on another story I'd heard a thousand
times.

"I have to go join the rest of the band," I said. "I'll see you after the game."

I headed toward the end of the bleachers where the band sat, but halfway there I heard someone call my name. Elena waved to me from where she stood with the rest of the cheerleaders, all wearing matching red-and-black uniforms.

"Hey," I said, walking over to her.

"Did you talk to Greg today?" Elena asked. "How is Lucas doing?"

I raised my eyebrows. "Do you really care?"

Elena looked hurt. "Yes, I care. Just because I broke up with him doesn't mean I want him to be miserable forever."

I remembered the furious look in Lucas's eyes earlier that afternoon. "He's upset, but he'll get over it." I hoped. I had been on edge since my run-in with the Spartans, and the worried feeling in my stomach would not go away.

Elena smiled. "He'll find someone who is perfect for him." She glanced toward the locker rooms, her smile widening. "Just like I did."

"Yeah," I said, rolling my eyes. "I'll see you after the game."

I made my way toward the bleachers, where people were already gathering to watch the kickoff. On the other side of the field, the Clark High School cheerleaders performed for a few people sitting in the visitors' bleachers.

The band launched into the Troy fight song and the football players came running onto the field. The crowd around us was on its feet, shouting and clapping and stomping. The cheerleaders jumped up and down, flipped along the grass, and cheered as the guys passed them, walking tall and steady like a band of warriors preparing for battle.

"We love you, Perry!" some girls behind me shouted.

The crowd booed as Clark High jogged onto the field.

Troy won the first kickoff, and Perry and the rest of the defensive line waited on the sidelines while Hunter and his offense took the field.

Despite the support from the crowd, Troy was down 3–14 by the end of the first half. Whenever I wasn't playing, my hands were gripped around my flute, so tight that I had imprints from the keys in my palms. I couldn't help worrying about my brothers whenever I watched a game. How could they stand to take those hits? Before halftime, Perry had been slammed into the ground by a Clark player twice his size. When he didn't immediately get up, Coach Wellens and a medic rushed onto the field to make sure he was okay. Although Perry wasn't always my favorite person in the world, I was happy to see him walk off the field unharmed.

I didn't know what went on in the locker room during halftime, but whatever it was, it got the Trojans fired up. The guys intercepted Clark's passes, tackled their runners to stop them from gaining yards, and made significant movement down the field.

And then a low murmur started up around me during the last two minutes of the game. Something toward the end of the field had caught a lot of people's attention. People were craning their necks and talking. I stood up a little in my seat to see.

A group of guys and girls were outside the waist-high chain-link fence. They wore the dark blue letterman jackets of Lacede High School. I strained to see who was there.

Lucas leaned on the fence next to Ackley and said something to him. Ackley nodded, his eyes still on the field.

And then I saw another face in the group that made me hold my flute in a death grip. Greg was there, standing next to Owen.

I could understand the football players coming to check out the game, but why was Greg with them?

By now a lot of other people had noticed the Spartans, too, including the cheerleaders and the Troy players on the sidelines. The cheerleaders kept looking at Lucas and his friends and then whispering to one another. The Troy football players paced a little and tried to look intimidating.

It felt as if the people around me were holding their breath, waiting for something to happen. The worried knot in my stomach tightened. The Lacede guys stared at the Trojans menacingly.

Now I actually wished the game clock wouldn't tick down so fast. I wanted the game to last forever to keep everyone occupied.

But eventually, the last second changed to zero and the horn sounded, indicating the end of the game. Clark High had not been able to get any more points during the second half. Troy had won 31–14.

The players who had been on the sidelines alerted Hunter to the presence of the Lacede players. Hunter stared at Lucas for a moment, until Coach Wellens ordered him to the locker room.

"Have a good night, everyone," Ms. Holloway said to us as we packed up our instruments.

I worked slowly, letting other people on the bleachers leave as I stayed seated and carefully put my flute back into its case. My parents wouldn't be waiting for me, since I had planned to go out with Elena and everyone after the game.

The Spartans remained at the fence, leaning casually against it as if being at Troy was something they did every day.

Several of the Troy spectators eyed the Lacede guys as they made their way down the bleachers. The cheerleaders stood in a tight group on the grass, glaring back at the Spartan girls. I figured the girls must have been Spartan cheerleaders who had come to terrorize their former leader at her new home.

As the crowd thinned, I picked up my flute case and walked down the bleachers to the group of Spartans.

"What are you doing here?" I asked, focusing on Lucas and Greg.

"I came to watch some football," Lucas said.

"You missed everything except the last two minutes," I pointed out.

"Just came to pay a little visit to our football friends," Lucas said, a crooked grin spreading across his face.

Greg glanced at Lucas, then looked at me. "Cassie, maybe you should go home."

I crossed my arms. "I am not leaving until all of you do. The game is over."

"Not quite," Lucas told me. "I have some business to attend to with your brother."

"Get out of here," Elena said, stepping up to my side.

"Look who it is, girls," said one of the Spartan girls, sneering at Elena. "The traitor herself."

Elena rolled her eyes. "I had no choice but to come to Troy. School rezoning, remember?"

"But you did have a choice who you decided to give your loyalty to," the cheerleader snapped.

"Here they come," Owen said in a low voice, looking over our shoulders.

I glanced behind me to see Perry and Hunter had emerged from the locker room, followed by the rest of the Troy players. They were headed across the field toward us.

Turning back around, I stared hard at Greg, pleading silently for him to talk some sense into his brother and go home.

Greg wouldn't make eye contact with me.

As the Trojans reached the fence separating them from the Spartans, more people had joined them. The cheerleaders stood behind the guys, along with a few other Troy students. There were about thirty Trojans compared to the fifteen Spartans standing with Lucas, but the Spartans didn't back down as the Trojans drew close.

"What do we have here?" Hunter asked. "A few wayward Spartans far from home?"

The Trojan cheerleaders giggled nervously as they watched the guys to see what they would do next.

Lucas stared at Perry, moving closer to the fence so that they stood only inches apart.

"We came to pay our respects," Lucas told him, "before we kill you on the field."

Perry snorted and the other Trojans laughed. "Why don't you back up your threats with action?" he asked. "Why wait for the field?"

Lucas stepped forward again, holding his arms out to each side. "Fine, let's settle things right now."

I noticed Perry's jaw twitch. Lucas was bigger than Perry was, and his entire body had tensed, as if waiting to jump on Perry at any moment.

Perry snorted again, grinning wide to his fans behind him as if Lucas's threats didn't bother him at all. But I knew him better than they did. Perry was nervous. All I had to do was see the way his nostrils flared slightly and how wide his eyes opened. He looked toward Hunter for reassurance.

"I'd hate to mess up your pretty face," Perry said, reaching out to pat Lucas's cheek over the fence.

Lucas slapped Perry's hand away, and Hunter stepped forward.

"You got a problem with my brother, take it up with me," Hunter said.

Ackley stared hard at Hunter, his hands curled into tight fists.

Lucas laughed, his eyes on Perry. "Going to let your brother fight your battles for you?"

"You're one to talk, Lucas," Elena said, her arms crossed over her chest. "How many times has Greg gotten you out of things?"

Lucas glared back at her in silence.

"At least I know how to be loyal to the people I care about," Greg said. "But you just run off with whoever happens to smile in your direction."

"Perry did not steal me away," Elena snapped. "Ask Cassie. She knows everything."

Oh, great. Thanks a lot, Elena.

Greg looked at me. "What does she mean?"

"Cassie knows I've been wanting to break up with Lucas for days," Elena said.

Something in Greg's eyes changed as he looked at me. His expression clouded over and the muscles in his forearms tightened.

Lucas looked as if he wanted to punch someone, and he probably would have, except that a shrill whistle suddenly sounded around us. I clasped my hands over my ears as Coach Wellens pushed himself in front of the fence, between the two guys. Ms. Holloway stood behind him along with some other teachers.

"What is going on here?" Coach Wellens asked, looking first at the Spartans and then at the Trojans.

Hunter's eyes were still on Lucas, but he stepped back and his shoulders relaxed slightly. "Nothing, Coach. Just having a little chat."

"How about you all save it for the field," Coach Wellens said. "Tonight's game is over. That means get off the school grounds and go home. If I hear there's been fighting, here or anywhere else, I will bench anyone involved for the rest of the season." He turned toward Lucas. "And don't think I can't have you Spartans benched as well. Coach Whittingham happens to be an old college buddy of mine."

No one moved. Lucas and Perry continued to stare at each other, as if silently daring the other to make the first move.

"Are you all hard of hearing?" Coach Wellens roared, spit flying from his mouth as he spoke. "I said it's time to go home. *Now!*"

The cheerleaders were the first to scurry away, followed by everyone else.

Ackley looked back at Hunter. "See you on the field, Prince," he growled.

I looked at Greg. He looked away. And followed his brother toward the parking lot.

THE TREES LOOKED LIKE GHOSTS.

At least, that was my first thought as my brothers' car rumbled down the road toward Troy High on Monday morning. The trees that stood outside on the front lawn were white and billowed in the morning breeze.

As the car drew closer, I saw that the billowy white was toilet paper. Long streamers of toilet paper hung from the branches and waved in the wind.

The trees weren't the only things that had been attacked by the toilet paper. The stone Trojan and his horse were now mummies, toilet paper streamers had been raised up the flagpole, and the maintenance workers were already gathering up the toilet paper that had been thrown across the front steps.

"Ugh," I said when I climbed out of the car. I pressed the back of my hand against my nose. "What is that smell?"

"Eggs," said Elena as she, Kelsey, and Mallory joined us. "There are eggs all over the front door and windows."

"Who did this?" Perry asked.

"Who do you think?" Kelsey said.

Something clicked in my head. "You don't think someone from Lacede did this?"

"Who else would do it?" Mallory snapped.

"How about any of the other schools we play against? Or maybe even someone who goes to Troy?"

"No," Hunter said in a low, even voice, "this was a Spartan attack."

Students were gathering around us, murmuring about their anger toward the Spartans. The rest of the football team had made their way to the front of the crowd, closest to Hunter, looking to him as if waiting for his command.

"What are we going to do?" Paul Baker asked.

"It's just a stupid prank," I said. "Can't we just forget it and worry about beating Lacede on the football field instead?"

My suggestion was met with loud disagreement.

"It's too late for that, Cassie," Hunter told me. "The Spartans have started a war. We can't back down without looking like the weaker team."

"Right," another football player agreed, pumping his fist into the air. His eyes shone, eager to get revenge. "We'll take down those Spartans and show them just who they're dealing with."

The rest of the students cheered, looking toward the football players as if they were gods. Perry, who had been standing with his arm slung around Elena and nuzzling her neck while Hunter talked, now stood straight and tall, basking in the attention from the other students.

"It's just a stupid rivalry," I muttered.

"Stupid or not," Perry said, "those Spartans won't get away with defacing our school."

Troy High buzzed with energy as everyone shouted about getting revenge.

"We will take those Spartans down," Hunter vowed.

The boys around him cheered, pumping their fists and grunting like apes. The girls clapped and bounced up and down, smiling wide.

Elena seemed at ease in the middle of this Spartan bashing. You wouldn't believe that she had ever set foot in Lacede High from the way she cheered right along with the Trojans.

"We are *so* going to get them," Elena said. "They'll regret messing with us."

"Are you forgetting you used to be a Spartan?" I asked.

Elena rolled her eyes. "I go to Troy now. I have to be loyal to my new school. I would think you'd be on our side too, since your brothers are leading this battle."

"Oh, I'm sorry," I said, "I didn't realize this was a *battle*. I thought it was just two schools playing dumb pranks on each other. Should I get out my armor and prepare for war?"

"You're such a brat, Cassie," Elena told me.

Immediately, I felt sorry for what I'd said. I hated the thought of Elena being annoyed with me.

"You're right," I said. "I'm a brat sometimes. Just ask my brothers."

A small smile twitched at the corners of Elena's mouth.

"I just wish our schools didn't have to hate each other so much," I said. "What is the point of this rivalry anyway? I mean, it's not like we have a choice about which school we attend. You should know that well enough."

"It's just a fun thing," Elena said. "It's called school spirit. You should try getting some every once in a while."

"Uses too much energy," I said.

◆ ◆ ◆

"Hey, honey," Mom greeted me as she looked up from her laptop, which sat open on the kitchen table. "Have fun at school?"

"A blast," I said, pulling the refrigerator open and

grabbing a bottle of Snapple. "Walked through rotten eggs, planned an attack on an enemy school, you know, the usual."

Mom looked up from her work. "What's this about an attack?"

I took a long drink of my Snapple. "Nothing," I said. I didn't want to explain about Lucas and Elena and Perry. I was tired of thinking about it and just wanted to forget it for a while. "I'm just kidding. My day was the typical American high school day. I'll let you get back to work."

I kissed Mom's cheek and headed toward my room. I closed my door and picked up my phone.

"Hello?" Greg said when he answered the phone.

"Hey," I greeted him. "Seen any good sales on toilet paper lately?"

Greg waited a second too long before saying, "What?"

"Someone toilet-papered and egged Troy High last night," I told him. "You wouldn't happen to know anything about that, would you?"

Greg made a grunting noise. "Why should I?"

I settled back on my bed. "Oh, I don't know. I just thought maybe Lucas had decided to get back at Perry and Elena by defacing our school. It sounds like something he'd do, you know?"

"Just because Lucas does something doesn't mean I'm involved."

"*Were* you involved?"

"You're so annoying sometimes, Cassie," Greg said, his voice tight.

"Just answer the question. Yes or no?"

"No, I wasn't involved!" Greg exclaimed. "Are you happy now?"

"A little," I said, "but I have one more question. Did you know about it?"

Greg was quiet for several moments. "It was just a prank."

"So you knew."

"And you knew Elena was going to dump Lucas."

We were both quiet for a long time, listening to each other breathing over the phone line.

"Are you done accusing me or is there something else you want to lay on me?"

I sighed. "Could you just ask Lucas not to do anything else? Some of the kids at Troy are talking about getting revenge."

"What are they planning?"

"I don't know," I said. "I hope they won't go through with it, whatever it is, but I'm afraid Lucas may have made things worse between our schools. Just ask him to stop."

"I can't promise that he'll listen to me."

"I know, but try. I'll talk to you later."

I hung up the phone and slumped back into my pillows. I'd known Lucas long enough to think this was only the beginning.

10

TROY GOT THEIR REVENGE THREE DAYS LATER.

I didn't see it, but I heard about it as soon as I arrived at the courtyard outside the gym Thursday morning.

"On the front of the school?" I heard Kelsey ask Mallory.

"All the way across the front," Mallory answered, nodding.

I looked to Elena for some clue as to what they were talking about, but she and Perry were busy cuddling and exchanging saliva.

"Serves them right, for starting the war," Kelsey said.

I raised an eyebrow at Hunter. "What did I miss?"

Perry heard me and broke away from Elena long enough to raise his fists in the air and shout, "Troy rules!"

"And Lacede drools, I know," I finished. "You could come up with something better than elementary school chants, you know."

"Oh, really?" Perry asked. "Hunter, show her."

Hunter reached into his pocket and produced some photographs. I took the photos, gasping as I looked through them.

"You spray-painted Lacede?" I asked, my voice rising in pitch.

The crowd sitting around the courtyard laughed as I stared down at the pictures of Lacede High, which featured the word LOSER painted in giant red letters over where it used it say LACEDE across the front of the school.

"Now everyone will know that the Spartans are nothing but losers," said Paul Baker, another football player.

I glared at Paul. "Lacede may have toilet-papered and egged our school, but they didn't spray-paint it. Do you realize how much it'll cost to clean this off?"

Paul pretended to wipe away a tear. "Oh, boo-hoo. Like I care."

"Lacede started this, Cassie," Hunter told me. "If your friend Lucas had been a man and left our school alone, we would never have had to deface his. If you're looking for someone to blame, look at your Spartan friends."

"Lucas is not my friend." I shoved the pictures back into Hunter's hand.

"You could have fooled us," Mallory said, crossing her arms over her chest. "You seemed to be pretty friendly with the Spartans at the game last Saturday. And we know you were at the Lacede game the night before."

"I'm friends with Lucas's brother," I said. "Is there a law against that?"

"You might want to reconsider who you're seen with these days, Cassie," Hunter told me. "I don't want someone getting the wrong idea and thinking you're a traitor to your school."

I heaved a long sigh. "Can we please grow up and forget this rivalry?"

Hunter shook his head, his expression serious. "Sorry, but things are already in motion. We can't back down now."

◆ ◆ ◆

"It's over now," Elena told me a week after Troy got revenge on Lacede. "Lacede attacked us, we attacked them, now we're even."

I hoped she was right. I hadn't heard a word from Greg. I had started to e-mail him several times, but I always deleted my half-finished e-mails without sending them. It wasn't that I worried about the other Trojans getting mad at me for talking to a Spartan, it was just that things were changing between us and I didn't know how to talk to him anymore. Kissing Greg was the biggest mistake I'd ever made. Everything started to unravel after that happened.

But then another part of me was glad I had kissed him. This same part of me wanted to run over to his house every afternoon and kiss him again and again. It was obviously the insanely masochistic side of me that hadn't been hurt enough by Greg's lack of enthusiasm for our first kiss.

I was tempted to beat my head against the wall just to try to get rid of the thoughts of him.

I sat down at my usual table during lunch that afternoon. Kelsey was out sick, so it was just Elena, Mallory, and me.

"This spaghetti looks disgusting," Mallory said, picking up the rubbery noodles with her fork.

I looked down at my own spaghetti. It really didn't look appetizing—watery sauce with a few shriveled meatballs—but I was starving. I'd slept late and hadn't been able to eat breakfast before school.

I shoved a huge forkful of spaghetti into my mouth.

"Ugh," Elena said as she watched me. She took dainty bites of her spaghetti.

Mallory made a face, but she cut up her noodles and ate the spaghetti also.

"Have you guys bought homecoming dresses yet?" Mallory asked. The homecoming game was still more than a month away, with the big dance in the school gym later that night.

Elena's eyes lit up. "Not yet. I'm still trying to decide on a color."

"I have a black dress with a jeweled neckline," Mallory said. "It needs to be hemmed a bit though."

"What about you?" Elena asked me.

I swallowed my mouthful of noodles. "Me? I don't go to dances."

The two girls stared at me as if I'd said I still believed in Santa Claus.

"This is not just a dance," Elena told me. "This is *homecoming*. You have to go."

"No, I don't. I don't dance and I don't get dressed up."

"You don't have to dance," Mallory said. "You just have to be there. *Everyone* is going."

"*Everyone*?" I asked, twirling my spaghetti around with my fork. "I doubt that. There has to be at least one other loser around here who would rather not spend their Friday night at school."

"It's not *school* when you're attending a dance," Elena

informed me. "You're going to homecoming. If you don't want to buy a dress, I have one you can borrow."

Elena had to be at least four inches taller than me. Even if by some miracle our waists were the same size, any dress of hers would make me look like a little kid dressing up in her mother's clothes.

"Thank you, but no. I'm not going."

"Yes, you are," said Elena. She squeezed my arm. "It'll be fun. Trust me."

Half an hour later, during my history class, my stomach gave a sudden rumble. I pressed my hand to my abdomen, feeling a little queasy.

Apparently, I wasn't the only one. Across the room, Keenan Willoughby raised his hand and said, "Mr. Tompkins? May I be excused?"

Mr. Tompkins stopped in the middle of his lecture on the Constitutional Congress and looked at Keenan. "You'll have to wait until the end of class."

Keenan bounced in his seat. "I don't think I can wait that long, sir."

A few seats behind him, Georgette Lipinski raised her hand. "I have to go too, Mr. Tompkins. It's an emergency." She sat slumped forward in her seat, clutching her stomach.

A few other kids raised their hands, asking to be excused.

And then I knew why they needed to be excused so suddenly. My stomach rumbled again and I realized I needed to get to a bathroom *right away*.

I raised my hand, joining the others pleading for Mr. Tompkins to let them out of class. Mr. Tompkins stared at us, his expression going between doubt to confusion. I knew it looked strange to him, that half of his class suddenly needed to use the bathroom at the same time, but I didn't think I could wait any longer.

Keenan definitely couldn't. He jumped up from his seat and ran to the door, pulling it open and dashing into the hall.

"Keenan, get back in here!" Mr. Tompkins exclaimed.

Now that Keenan had acted, the rest of us didn't waste time either. We tripped over backpacks in our haste to get out.

In the hall, other classrooms were open as well, with students running out and teachers calling after them to come back. I saw a few teachers also running with us, everyone clutching their stomachs and moving as fast as their legs would carry them, trying to get to a bathroom stall before they were all taken.

◆ ◆ ◆

I felt better but not fully back to normal that night when Elena insisted I go out to the Ice Cream Factory with her and a bunch of other kids from school. Of course, Perry and Hunter were going, so I rode with them, squished into the back of their car between Elena and Mallory.

The Ice Cream Factory was pretty busy. So busy that we didn't notice the crowd in blue letterman jackets that had walked in the door until the whispers reached our table.

Several members of the Spartan football team stood just inside the restaurant, with Lucas and Ackley in the front. On the edge of the group stood Greg. His eyes met mine briefly before he looked away.

Perry was the first of our group to stand. "What have we here?" he asked, giving a sly grin. "Lost Spartans? Need a hand finding your way back home?"

Lucas stepped forward, his fists clenched. "Need a hand rearranging your face?"

Perry's grin faltered a bit.

"Are you going to let him talk to you like that?" Hunter asked our brother, pushing him in the small of his back toward Lucas. Hunter had been even grumpier than usual all afternoon, a side effect of the stomach problems, I assumed.

Perry laughed. "I wouldn't want to injure him right in the middle of football season," he said. "Who else is better to lead Loser High's team to defeat?"

Behind Lucas, Owen looked tense and ready to pounce. Greg stood silent and still, watching the scene with a scowl on his face. Ackley had his usual glare directed at Hunter, and at his side his best friend, Patrick, snickered in my brother's direction.

"Besides," Perry said, "this isn't the place to fight. Let's leave it to the field."

"Let's do it right now," Patrick said, stepping toward Hunter.

Hunter stood from his seat to stare down at Patrick, but Ackley stepped forward so that he was eye to eye with Hunter. Neither of them moved, their bodies tensed.

"Let's say that the team with the most wins at the end of the season is the most dominant team," Lucas suggested. "We'll settle the rivalry once and for all."

The Trojans and Spartans murmured among themselves, most nodding in agreement.

And then a gleam came into Lucas's eye. His next words startled all of us.

"I hear there's a nasty stomach virus going around Troy."

Hunter turned away from Ackley and scowled at Lucas. "What is that supposed to mean, Spartan?"

Lucas shrugged. "Nothing. Just a virus, right? I'm sure you'll all be back to normal very soon."

Now the other Trojans stood up as well.

"If you know something about what made half of our school sick today," Paul Baker said, "I suggest you 'fess up and save yourself from a worse beating."

"Relax," Greg said, rolling his eyes. "It was just laxatives in the spaghetti sauce. It's not like it's going to kill you."

I stared at him, my heart sinking to my toes. He still didn't meet my gaze.

Every muscle in Hunter's face twitched. "And just how did you get laxatives into the spaghetti?"

Ackley smiled. "That's our little secret."

I didn't see who made the first move, but the next thing I knew, a fight had broken out between the Spartans and Trojans. Someone fell against my chair, causing me to fall forward and slam my knees into the tile floor. I heard Elena shriek near me and then saw her get swept up into Perry's arms.

I crawled under the table for cover while the guys from both teams pushed one another around, swinging arms and legs. Ackley ran at Hunter, pushing him backward into a booth.

It wasn't long before the employees of the Ice Cream Factory broke up the fight, but it felt like forever as I crouched under the table with Mallory and a few other girls.

"Break it up right now or I'm calling the cops!" shouted Bennie, the big, burly cook. The room got quiet and I came out of my hiding place to see Hunter and the rest of the Trojan football team standing on one side of the room with Greg and Lucas and the rest of the Spartans on the other. Bennie stood between them, his arms raised as he looked back and forth between the two groups. "I want all of you out of here right now. If you're not off this property in five seconds, I'm calling the police."

Lucas wiped at his bloody nose with the back of his hand. Greg looked at his brother, then back at Hunter. Greg's eyes were dark and his face stony.

"You'll pay, Prince," Ackley said, pointing at my brother. He helped Patrick, who had a huge red welt forming on the side of his face, to get up, and they turned toward the door.

Greg didn't even look at me as he led his brother out of the restaurant.

Bennie pointed toward us. "I mean all of you. Out!"

Hunter stomped toward the door and we all followed him. I thought the Spartans would be waiting outside to jump us, but I saw them speed away in their cars as we walked out into the parking lot.

Perry and Elena were sitting on the curb, Perry's arm wrapped around her shoulders.

"That was crazy," Perry said, grinning up at us.

Hunter snapped. "Crazy? What was crazy was how as soon as someone started swinging, you ran out here like a baby."

Perry jumped to his feet. "I was trying to get Elena out of the middle of the fight. I didn't want her to get hurt."

Hunter waved a hand toward where I stood shivering slightly from the cool night air and the aftershock of what had just happened. "Way to have concern for our sister's safety too, hero."

Perry looked me up and down. "She looks fine."

"You are such a brat," Hunter grunted, shoving Perry's chest and causing him to stumble backward a few steps. "This entire fight is because of you! And you won't even stand up and help out. You expect the rest of us to get hurt because of something *you* started while you sit back and make out with the girl you stole."

"Perry didn't steal me," Elena objected.

I would have told her that Hunter wasn't listening to a word she said, but I was too afraid to speak or move. No one else moved either, as we watched my brothers in the light of the streetlamps.

"This is your fault, Perry," Hunter growled, pointing a thick finger in Perry's face. "And you *are* going to help end it. I don't care if your pretty little face gets messed up. You will fight your own battle. Got it?"

For a moment, I thought Perry might stand up to Hunter. No one ever had. But he backed down.

"Got it," he said. He turned and reached a hand out to Elena. "Come on, let's get out of here."

11

THE NEXT MORNING, I STILL FELT A LITTLE
shaken by what had happened at the Ice Cream Factory.
I hadn't slept well, remembering the look in Hunter's and
Greg's eyes. I knew Hunter could have a gruff attitude
when needed—he used it to rally the football team before
big games—but I had never seen that side of Greg before.
The look on his face when he saw that Lucas had been
injured frightened me.

This war wouldn't end soon; I could feel that deep in
my gut.

During the short time that I did manage to sleep, I
dreamed about Hunter. I saw him on the football field,
dodging around other players who were coming after him.
I couldn't tell what school the players were from because

they were dressed all in black. In my dream, one of the enemy players suddenly grew huge and ran full speed at Hunter. The player rammed my brother hard, sending him spinning into the air, where he stayed suspended for what felt like hours. Suddenly, Hunter fell, crashing hard into the ground on his neck and shoulder.

Then my brother lay there, not moving at all.

I awoke sweating and panting heavily, as if I'd been the one running from the football players. My stomach churned and I couldn't get rid of the feeling that my dream had been a sort of warning.

I got ready for school as the memories of the night's events played through my mind again. When I went downstairs to breakfast, Hunter sat alone in the kitchen, reading the sports section while he ate his cereal.

"Hey," he greeted me, not looking up from the newspaper.

"Hey," I said. I got a bowl and spoon and then sat down at the table. But I didn't reach for the cereal. I just sat there, staring down into my empty bowl.

"Hunter?" I said after a moment.

He grunted in response, still not looking at me.

"Is this thing between the two schools really so important?" I asked. I didn't want to rile Hunter up first thing in the morning, but someone had to talk some sense into him. "I mean, it's just football."

Hunter looked at me, his gray eyes sad. "It's not just football, Cass. It's reputation and pride. Now it's personal. If we back down, we're saying that we're too afraid to stand up to them. The Spartans will never let us forget it. And we won't be the only ones who have to deal with it, everyone who attends Troy High in the future will. You think the rivalry is bad now, think about what would happen if we gave up without a fight."

I sighed. "But this is so stupid. Why can't our two schools just be friends?"

"That's just not the way it works around here," Hunter told me.

We were quiet for a moment and I poured Frosted Flakes into my bowl. Then I said, "Why are you leading this thing if it's between Perry and Lucas?"

Hunter gave me a look. "Do you honestly think Perry could lead anything?"

I remembered how he'd run out of the fight as fast as he could the night before. "No," I admitted. "He'd make an even bigger mess."

"Exactly. So I have no choice but to be the leader."

Hunter finished the rest of his cereal, slurping down the last of the milk in his bowl, and then stood to put his dishes in the sink. He turned back to me, smiling sadly.

"I hope you understand that I have to do this, Cassie,"

he said. "It's not that I hate your friend Greg or anything, it's just something that has been building between our two schools for years. Perry put this in motion, and I can't be the one to back down without losing the respect of all Trojans and Spartans. I don't want to do that to everyone at our school. Okay?" He reached over and touched my cheek gently, rubbing his thumb over my skin.

I nodded. "Okay. Just be careful. I had this dream. You got hurt on the field. Like, seriously hurt." Tears stung my eyes as I remembered the sight of my brother lying still and pale on the grass.

"It was just a dream," Hunter said. "But I promise I'll be careful. And you do the same. I know you care about Greg, but this is not the time to be seen running around town with him."

Judging from the way Greg had looked at me at the Ice Cream Factory, that didn't seem to be a likely option. A lump formed in my throat at this thought, but I nodded to my brother and tried to look as if my heart wasn't breaking into a million pieces.

◆ ◆ ◆

That night, Troy was winning 21–7 against Sunset High School. I tugged at the collar of my band uniform as I waited for time to tick down on the scoreboard. We had less than two minutes left in the fourth quarter. There was no way Sunset could catch up. People in the bleachers had already started to celebrate while the cheerleaders threw one another into the air to keep the enthusiasm up.

Hunter had played a great game. I wasn't sure if it was just his natural talent or if it had something to do with the aggression that coursed through him thanks to the Spartans, but he threw perfect passes and avoided the Sunset players whenever they came at him. Perry didn't do so bad either, but he seemed more interested in watching Elena bounce around in her cheerleading uniform than in actually focusing on the game.

Still, the crowd loved my brothers and the rest of the Troy team. They had cheered until they were hoarse, and the bleachers vibrated from their celebratory stomping.

When the last seconds ticked away and the horn sounded, ending the game, the Troy spectators flooded the field to hoist the football players onto their shoulders. Hunter pulled his helmet off and his light brown hair shone from the lights surrounding the field. People looked at him as if he were a soldier returning home victorious from a great war.

I made my way through the crowd toward the girls' locker room. Elena, Perry, Hunter, and some others were all going out to celebrate after the game and Elena had insisted I come, too. I didn't understand why she needed me to come along with her anymore, now that she and Perry were obviously together. She couldn't still be nervous around him and need my support.

Yet it felt strange to think that she might really, honestly want to be my friend. Since Elena's arrival, I almost felt like I was a part of something.

I pushed open the door to the girls' room and then froze, staring at the sight before me.

The lockers along the walls were open and everything had been pulled out and thrown all over the place. Red streaks covered all the clothes and bags, and the sinks and toilets had been stopped up with big bunches of toilet paper so that the water overflowed onto the floor.

I heard the cheerleaders approaching the locker room behind me.

"Hey, Cassie," said Elena. "Are you ready—"

She stopped halfway through the door and saw the mess around the room. The other girls crowded inside, staring openmouthed at the damage.

"What happened?" Mallory asked, turning to me.

I shook my head. "It was like this when I got here."

She looked at me suspiciously, until Kelsey pointed to the mirror over the sinks. "Look."

Written in red lipstick was the word *TRAITOR*.

"Spartans," one of the cheerleaders muttered, wrinkling her nose.

"Spartan cheerleaders," Elena corrected her. "Coming after me."

"How did they get in here?" Kelsey asked.

"The door wasn't locked," I said. "Remember, Ms. Fisher unlocked it before the game so we could go in and out? I don't think she locked it back up when the game started." Ms. Fisher was the cheerleading coach and the keeper of the girls' locker-room keys.

Mallory clenched her fists. "Oh, I wish I'd seen them when they snuck in. I would love to rip out some Spartan cheerleader hair."

Kelsey had moved toward her duffel bag and bent down to examine the red streaks all over it. "Ketchup," she said. "At least it'll wash out. But all our things are covered in it."

Elena turned toward the door, pushing through the other cheerleaders.

"Where are you going?" I asked.

"To find Perry," she said. "We're not just standing by and letting them get away with this."

12

I DIDN'T TALK TO GREG AT ALL THAT WEEKEND. I was angry at him for getting involved in the rivalry, but even more so about the fact that he obviously didn't want to be more than friends. Lately, I didn't feel that we were even friends at all. My wounded pride wouldn't ever allow me to make the first move again.

And if he really was a friend to me, he should have warned me about the laxatives in the spaghetti. He didn't even care enough to do that.

Since I hadn't talked to Greg in several days, I was surprised to see an e-mail from him appear in my inbox Monday afternoon.

TO: CassDestruction@troyhigh.edu

FROM: GMennon711@lacedehigh.edu

SUBJECT: Hope the Trojans are pleased with themselves...

ATTACHMENT: lacede.jpg

I opened the picture attached to the e-mail.

The photo showed the Lacede High football field. The grass had brown words burned into the green that spelled out YOU'LL REGRET THIS, SPARTANS.

◆ ◆ ◆

"Don't forget to read chapters four and five in *Of Mice and Men*," Mr. Sale said as the bell rang and students jumped from their seats. "I can't make any promises, but there just may be a quiz on the reading. So take my advice and be prepared. See you all tomorrow."

I shoved my English book into my backpack, along with my copy of *Of Mice and Men*, and slung my backpack over my shoulder.

"Ugh," Elena said. "Like we don't have anything else to do other than read books for English class. I have cheerleading practice every day this week."

"Yeah," I said, only half listening.

I couldn't get my mind off Greg. I had been thinking about him ever since I'd gotten his e-mail. It had been two weeks since we'd talked. We'd never gone this long without speaking.

I missed him, I thought, as I stepped into the hall. I missed our all-day video game sessions and jokes. And at night I dreamed about kissing him again.

I woke from the dreams sweating and out of breath.

A shriek from around the corner startled me out of my thoughts. The shriek turned into several screams and then squawks.

Squawks? Like birds?

The people in front of me jumped out of the way and a flash of brown feathers flew at me, wings flapping. Elena and I screamed and ducked, covering our heads. When I managed to lift my head up to see what was happening, I spotted a chicken running through the hall behind me.

More squawks made me turn around, and I saw several chickens, some white and others brown, dashing around legs and backpacks and running through the halls of Troy High.

"Catch them!" someone yelled.

A few of the guys were brave enough to dive at the chickens, but the birds flapped their wings and leaped out of their grasp. Now the shrieks and squawks were joined by shouts as the chickens tried to get away.

"How did chickens get into the school?" Elena cried, her eyes wide.

I had a sudden thought and pushed through the crowd

toward the front doors. I managed to get outside and hurried down the steps, scanning the parking lot.

There, on the road, Lucas's car turned the corner, following an old, rusty pickup truck full of metal cages.

◆ ◆ ◆

It took teachers and students two hours to catch all the chickens. When they were done and someone had been called to come pick them up, the hall was littered with textbooks, paper, feathers, and chicken droppings. It took another hour for maintenance to clean up and scrub the floors.

An emergency assembly had been arranged that afternoon in the school auditorium. The entire student population was forced to attend.

Ms. Fillmore, the Troy High principal, stood onstage behind a large wooden podium. She looked over the crowd, eyeing all of us for a long time before she began speaking.

"As I'm sure most of you are aware, there has been a rash of pranks played between our school and Lacede High," she said, her voice echoing throughout the room.

"Lacede sucks!" someone yelled. A bunch of people laughed and cheered.

Ms. Fillmore stared at us again, waiting until everyone had grown silent before she continued. "These pranks are against school policy," she said. "The destruction of school property is punishable by law. Let me warn all of you that pranks are not condoned and will not be tolerated. The guilty parties will be punished when they are caught. And believe me, they *will* be caught.

"I also must warn you," Ms. Fillmore said, "that fights at school games will not be tolerated. Visitors to our premises, even visitors from another school, are to be considered our guests while they are here and we will all treat them with respect and courtesy. Any student caught fighting on school grounds will face suspension.

"If anyone knows anything about the incidents of the last few weeks, please do not hesitate to come see me," she went on. "My office is always open and you will remain anonymous. Any information you can provide to help us stop these pranks and punish the offenders will be appreciated."

She stared around the room again, as if waiting for someone to speak up and confess to the pranks right then. I shifted in my seat as her eyes passed over me.

"Thank you all," Ms. Fillmore said at last. "You may return to your classes."

The room erupted into talk and laughter as everyone stood and started toward the doors.

I hung back, walking slowly in the crowd. The administration office was right outside the auditorium. Through the open door I could see the school secretary inside, sitting in front of her computer. Behind her was Ms. Fillmore's office.

I stared at the door, chewing my lower lip.

I could tell Ms. Fillmore everything. I could make it stop.

I would get Greg into trouble.

I would get my brothers into trouble.

Even I would get in trouble.

I hitched my backpack farther up my shoulder and looked at Ms. Fillmore's office again.

Then I turned around and headed back to class.

13

"WE HAVE TO TALK," HUNTER SAID, CORNERING me at home the next morning.

I tried to push past him, but he blocked my way to the bathroom. "I have to get ready for school," I said.

"This will just take a minute," he told me. "I don't want you to see that Greg Mennon again. Got it?"

I looked at Hunter as if he had lost his mind. "What?"

"I've been giving this a lot of thought and it's not a good idea for you two to be friends right now. Don't call or see him or anything."

He must have fallen out of bed during the night and hit his head. He couldn't possibly think that he had any right to tell me who I could or couldn't be friends with.

"Greg is my best friend," I said.

"You two haven't been much of best friends lately," Hunter said, crossing his arms. "Usually you're at his house all the time, but in the last few weeks you haven't even mentioned him. Did something happen? Has he hurt you?"

What happened was that I acted like an idiot and kissed him. But there was no way I was telling my brother about that.

"Nothing happened," I said. "But if I want to see Greg, I will. You can't stop me."

"I'm trying to protect you," Hunter said. "I've heard some of the other guys on the team talking and they don't like that my sister hangs out with a Spartan. Do you want people to think you're passing along information to the enemy? Do you want them to think you're not on our side?"

"I'm not," I said. "I'm not on anyone's side."

Perry's bedroom door opened and he walked into the hall, his cell phone pressed to his ear. "I miss you too, snuggle bear," he cooed.

Snuggle bear? Gag me.

Hunter snatched the phone out of Perry's hand and hung it up.

"Hey!" Perry exclaimed.

"You can talk to your girlfriend at school," Hunter

said. "Right now you need to help me talk some sense into our sister."

"What crawled into your Frosted Flakes and died?" Perry muttered. He looked at me. "Why does Cassie need sense talked into her this time?"

"She refuses to stop seeing that Spartan."

A slow grin spread across Perry's face. "Oh, you mean her boyfriend who she won't admit is her boyfriend?"

I gave Perry a quick punch in his side, causing him to double over and moan. "Both of you need to back off of me. I'll be friends with whomever I choose. Fight your stupid battle, but leave me out of it." I marched into the bathroom, slamming the door behind me.

"You're a part of it whether you want to be or not," Hunter called after me. "You're a Trojan."

◆ ◆ ◆

I was so tired of all the stupid games that people at Troy and Lacede were playing.

Greg and I had been friends for more than two years. It was stupid to let this school rivalry tear us apart.

After I got home from band practice that afternoon, I jumped on my bike and headed over to Greg's house. It was time to end this not-talking-to-each-other thing. I didn't want to lose my best friend, or whatever else we could be to each other.

Greg opened the door at my knock. He stared at me without saying a word.

"Hi." I shifted my weight from one foot to the other. "Look, I'm really sorry about how things have been between us. This rivalry has taken over everything. But it's not important and it's not our fight. I want us to be friends again."

Greg didn't say anything for a few moments.

Finally he spoke. "We were always still friends. Even if I'm mad at you, I haven't stopped being your friend."

I smiled. "I'm glad. Because I don't want to lose you."

Greg looked at me with a strange look in his eye. For some reason, it made me blush.

"I don't want to lose you, either," he told me. He stepped back and held the door open wider. "Do you want to come in?"

I stepped into the house. "So where is Lucas? I don't see his car outside."

Greg gave me an annoyed look. "If you're wondering whether he's out planning any more pranks against Troy, he's not. He and my dad went fishing."

"Lucas fishes?" I asked incredulously.

"No, he doesn't. But my dad talked him into going. My parents thought it might be good for Lucas to get out and do something relaxing. Dad offered to take me, too, but I told him I had a lot of studying to do." Greg grinned. "Fishing's not really my thing."

We went to the den. Greg picked up his game controller and pressed the Start button to continue the video game he was playing. I sat on the couch and watched him play in silence for a while, sneaking glances at his profile every now and then. I liked the curves of his face and his strong jawline. I liked the way his bottom lip stuck out just a little farther than the top.

I was in love with my best friend.

I shook my head and pressed the palms of my hands into my eyes.

"You okay?" Greg asked.

I opened my eyes to see a fuzzy shape leaning close to me. After blinking a few times, the image came into focus and I could see Greg's concerned face.

"I'm fine," I said. "Just a little tired. I haven't slept well lately."

Greg frowned. "Neither have I."

What did he mean by that? Had he not slept well because he worried about the rivalry? Or had he not slept well because he was thinking about me?

I had to change the subject. "Hunter told me this morning that I had to stop being friends with you."

Greg raised his eyebrows. "He did *what*?"

"He says he's worried about me, but I kind of think he's just worried about how it makes him look. You know, that his own sister hangs out with a Spartan."

"Did he threaten you?" Greg scowled.

"My brother wouldn't threaten me," I said. "Anyway, he has a lot to learn if he thinks he can push me around. That was what made me decide to come here and make things right between us. You know when someone tells me not to do something, I do it anyway." I grinned.

But Greg didn't smile back. He looked annoyed as he punched at the buttons on his controller. "I can't believe he said that," he muttered. "Hunter can do whatever he wants to me or Lucas, but he better leave you out of it."

His tone made me nervous. But I decided to change the subject again.

"So the Troy homecoming game is about a month away," I said. "There's going to be a dance after, and everyone tells me that I *have* to go because everyone else does and it'll be the first dance I've ever attended and maybe you could come with me?"

I stopped, horrified at the words that had just spilled out of my mouth. I hadn't meant to say that.

Greg looked at me, his eyebrows raised. "You want me to go to a dance at *Troy*?"

My neck grew hot and I stared at the floor. "No," I said.

"I mean, not unless you want to. It's just a stupid dance. Forget I mentioned it. Elena has been talking my ear off about it for the last couple of weeks and apparently we'd have to get dressed up if we went."

Greg was silent. I knew he didn't want to go. Why would he want to go to a dance? With *me*? I should have kept my mouth shut and saved us both from the agony of another uncomfortable moment.

"Are you sure I should go?" Greg asked. "I mean, the guys at Troy don't really like Lacede guys very much right now."

"Well, you going could help them see that you're not the enemy," I said slowly.

What was I doing? Why was I trying to convince Greg to go to a dance? As my date?

"But you don't have to," I forced myself to add. "We can do something else that night, like go to the movies or play video games."

Greg paused his game as he chewed his lower lip. "Okay," he said after a moment. "I'll go to the dance with you."

I couldn't have heard him right. "Huh?"

"I said I'll go to homecoming with you. I'll be your date."

My heart pounded against my ribs as his words sunk

in. He had said "date." He was going to be my date to the dance.

"Wait," I said suddenly. "You're not going so you can play a prank against Troy at the dance, are you?"

Greg scowled. "I'm going as your date because you asked me to, that's it. We're going to dance and have a good time. And hopefully the guys at Troy will see that Spartans are not so bad and will back off."

I smiled. "Okay. Thanks."

He smiled back at me. "No problem. That's what friends do, right?"

I tried not to let my face show my pain at the word "friends."

"That's right," I said.

Greg unpaused his game and turned back to the TV.

"You know," I said after a moment, "the chickens in the school were pretty funny."

Greg didn't look away from the TV, but I saw the corners of his lips turn up into a grin.

14

"I DON'T UNDERSTAND WHY WE'RE SHOPPING already," I said as I pushed aside dresses that were too frilly, too pink, too revealing, too not-me.

"You can never start shopping too early," Elena told me. She took a pale yellow, gauzy gown from the rack and held it up to her body in front of the mirror on the wall. "What do you think?"

Mallory looked up from the rack she was browsing through and said, "The yellow blends in with your hair too much. I think you should go with a blue."

Elena ran her hand over the fabric wistfully, then nodded. "You're right. I love the dress, but it's not really my color." She put it back on the rack, still frowning.

This was why I didn't like shopping. I had no idea

what my colors were. And everything in Gina's Formal Wear just looked . . . well, too formal. I wasn't the type of girl who liked to get all dressed up and get her hair and makeup done. I was a jeans and T-shirt girl. I wore my long, brown hair either loose or in a ponytail. And I had absolutely no clue what to do with makeup.

But I couldn't admit that to Elena, Mallory, and Kelsey. They would think I was even more of a loser than they already did.

I hadn't told them yet that Greg was my date to homecoming. If I thought my lack of girlyness would freak them out, telling them that I was bringing a Spartan to a Troy dance would very likely give them strokes. And besides, I wasn't too eager for my brothers to find out.

"Found anything you like yet?" Elena asked me.

I pretended to look through the gowns in front of me. "No," I said. "Nothing is really my style."

"Don't be ridiculous," Elena said. She reached past me and pulled out an emerald-green satin gown with spaghetti straps and a row of sequins along the neckline. "This dress was made for you. This color would be gorgeous with your hair and eyes."

"Definitely," Kelsey spoke up from a couple of racks away.

The dress was pretty, but I still wasn't sold. "Aren't these straps a little thin?"

"Cassie," Mallory said, "no offense, but you really don't have much up top that big straps need to hold in place. The spaghetti straps are fine."

Why couldn't the floor open up and swallow me right then?

"Just try it on," Elena urged me. "You won't know how it looks until you see yourself in it."

"Fine," I said, grabbing the dress from her hands and hurrying toward the dressing rooms.

Once I had locked myself in a stall, I pulled off my sneakers and clothes. I just wanted to get this shopping trip over with. It really didn't matter to me what I wore to the dance, because I felt too nervous about going with Greg to put much focus on my wardrobe. Just as long as I didn't look completely stupid, I couldn't care less what I wore.

After I'd slipped the gown on, I turned around to look in the mirror on the back of the door. What I saw reflected back stunned me. I didn't look like the regular Cassie Prince, I looked more like Elena. Well, of course I didn't look *exactly* like Elena, but I looked like the kind of girl she was. The kind of girl who could kiss a guy and he would actually like it.

Elena was right, the color suited me. It brought out the tiny green flecks in my gray eyes and made my dark hair look warmer. The dress fit me perfectly, revealing a waistline that I had never really noticed before.

A knock sounded on the door. "Come on out," Elena called. "We want to see."

I opened the door and stepped out of the dressing room, ducking my head so that my hair fell in front of my eyes. I felt a bit embarrassed standing there being scrutinized by them.

"Well?" I asked.

Elena clapped her hands, grinning wide. "Oh, Cassie, you look beautiful!" she said. "You're a Trojan princess."

"People at school will be amazed when they see you," Mallory told me, nodding her approval.

"You should wear your hair up," Kelsey said, reaching out to twist my long hair up toward my head. "To show off your shoulders. Guys love that."

For the first time, as I looked at our reflections in the mirrored wall, I felt like I really was one of them. Like I actually fit in.

I had never realized how much I had missed out on, being a loner at Troy and not having girlfriends to hang out with. It was nice having three girls fuss over me and argue about how I should wear my hair and makeup.

Maybe, if I could learn from them about how to be a

girl, the next time I kissed a boy he would want to kiss me back.

*   *   *

After we were done at Gina's, we headed over to the mall food court for a snack. We had just gotten milk shakes and were headed toward the benches in the center of the mall to sit, when Mallory stopped suddenly.

"Spartans," she whispered.

We saw them at the same time they saw us. Lucas turned around and said something to the others with him—Greg, Owen, Ackley, Patrick, and a couple other guys from the football team—and then they turned in our direction.

"Ugh," Elena muttered. "I do not want to deal with him right now."

But Lucas sauntered toward us across the tile floor, his eyes locked on Elena.

"Hello, traitor," he greeted her.

Elena rolled her eyes. "What do you want, Lucas?"

Lucas shrugged. "Nothing, we just came by to say hi."

"Hi," she said. "Now, if you'll excuse us, we were just leaving—"

Elena tried to step around him, but Owen moved into her path. The other guys fanned out to form a half-circle around us. Greg stood at Lucas's side and refused to look at me.

"We haven't had a chance to talk in such a long time, Elena," Lucas said. "Not without your pretty boyfriend present."

"We don't have anything to talk about," Elena said. "We broke up."

"No," Lucas told her, his voice low. "*We* didn't. *You* did."

"Greg," I said, reaching out to touch his arm. "Don't let him do this."

Lucas sneered at me. "What's wrong, Cassie? Afraid?"

Greg stepped forward between Lucas and me, facing his brother. "Hey," he said. "Leave her out of this. Say what you want to Elena and then let's go."

Lucas stared at his brother for a moment, but Greg didn't back down. Finally, Lucas turned back to Elena.

"After everything we've been through," he said to her, "I can't believe you would run off with the first coward who would smile in your direction."

"Coward?" Mallory said, stepping next to Elena. "You're calling Perry a coward?"

Lucas looked around. "I don't see him anywhere, standing up for his girl. The only thing I've seen Perry Prince do is run away as fast as he can as soon as the action starts. He doesn't want to mess up his pretty-boy looks. I call that being a coward."

"Perry was protecting Elena," Kelsey said.

Lucas looked back at the other guys and they laughed, all except Greg, who stood tense.

"Keep telling yourself that," Lucas said. "Keep pretending Perry is some great hero instead of the sniveling baby he really is." He punched his fist into his other hand. "If he was here right now, I'd—"

"What?" said a deep voice behind the Spartans. "What would you do?"

Lucas and the other Spartans spun around to see Hunter standing behind them. None of us had noticed him approaching. Even alone, he gave off an aura of strength and power as he stared down at the Spartans.

"What were you saying?" Hunter asked, his glare locked on Lucas.

There was a moment of silence, and then Lucas seemed to regain his composure. He stepped forward, but then Greg and Owen grabbed his arms, pulling him back.

"Are you insane?" Owen asked. "That guy is twice your size. He'll stomp you into a pulp."

Lucas wrenched his arms free. "I'm not afraid of him. Or his coward brother."

"Neither am I," Patrick said, stepping forward toward Hunter even though my brother towered over him by several inches.

Ackley grabbed his best friend's arm. "Back off, Patrick.

If anyone's going to do this, it'll be me. It's payback time."
He curled his hands into fists as he sneered at my brother.

Hunter looked at each of the Spartans in silence, then he looked past them to me. "Cassie, you okay?" he asked. "Are they bothering you?"

I swallowed hard. I knew Elena and the girls wanted me to say yes so that Hunter would save the day and get rid of them for us. But I couldn't give him a reason to go after Greg.

"We're okay," I said. "We're done now."

Hunter nodded once and I grabbed Elena's arm, pulling her away with Mallory and Kelsey following. I looked over my shoulder to see Lucas watching us leave.

15

"WELL, IF IT ISN'T GREG THE SILENT." I SLID INTO the booth Greg occupied at TJ's.

He looked startled to see me. "What are you doing here?"

"I went by your house and your mom said you would be here." I picked up the menu and scanned over the items I knew by memory. "I'm hungry anyway. I could use a cheeseburger."

"Actually," Greg said, "I was just leaving."

I raised an eyebrow at him. "But you haven't eaten yet. Have you ordered already?"

"I'm not hungry," Greg said. "I just came in here to get a glass of water. I'm headed to the library now. I have a really big project to research."

Yeah, I didn't believe that for one minute. Why come all the way to TJ's, which was three blocks farther from his house than the library, just for a glass of water?

Something else was going on, and I wanted to know what it was.

Greg stood and started putting on his jacket. I looked up at him and asked, "Are you trying to get rid of me?"

Greg tried to look innocent. "Why would I be doing that?"

"Why don't you tell me?" I asked. "Since you're the one trying to get rid of me."

"I'm not. I really have to go to the library. I have a huge history paper due next week."

I rolled my eyes. "Fine, whatever. Just stop freaking out." I slid out of the booth and stood up next to him, so close that I could smell mints on his breath.

"I'm not freaking out."

"You're certainly acting really weird," I said. "What's gotten into—"

"Hey, Greg," said a voice behind us.

I turned around and looked into the big green eyes of a tall, pretty brunette. Was this why Greg wanted me gone? Was he on a *date*?

But then I noticed two other girls and a guy behind her.

"Hey, guys," Greg greeted them.

"Are we early?" one of the other girls asked, pushing past me to slide into the booth. She carried a laptop that she set on the table and opened.

Greg shook his head. "No, you're right on time."

The first girl who had spoken, the brunette, stared hard at me. "Don't I know you from somewhere?" she asked.

I shook my head. "I don't think so—"

"She's a Trojan," the girl with the laptop said, her gaze still on the screen. "Cassie Prince, younger sister of Hunter and Perry Prince." She looked at me, smiling at my look of surprise. "I make it my business to get to know all the key players on the enemy side."

They all glared at me, then at Greg.

"Hanging out with the enemy?" the guy said.

"Lay off it, Kevin," Greg told him. "Cassie and I have been friends for years. She's not part of this rivalry."

"Her brothers are the ones leading the attacks against us," Kevin snapped. "She's as much a part of it as any of us. And I have to say, Greg, it doesn't look very good to have our class president being seen in public with a Trojan."

Greg stood straighter, holding his shoulders back as he stared Kevin down. "Are you going to do something about it? You're class *vice* president, not president, remember?"

Even though I worried a little that Kevin might do

something, I had to admit that Greg looked really hot when he was defending my honor.

"Come on, guys," said laptop girl from her seat in the booth. "We have a lot of work to go over and I have to be home in an hour. Have your macho showdown some other time."

The guys stared at each other a moment longer, then Kevin slid into the booth with the other two girls sliding in next to him.

"Tell Elena Argos that Spartans don't forget people who betray them," the brunette girl told me, her face twisted into a sneer.

Greg grabbed my arm and steered me toward the door. "I'll talk to you later, Cassie," he told me.

"Okay" was all I managed to say before he led me out the door and then returned to his student council friends.

◆ ◆ ◆

"We have to get them back," Kelsey said, three days later, thumping her fist on Elena's desk.

We had gathered in Elena's room after school. I laid on Elena's white ruffled comforter, staring up at the ceiling where she'd stuck glow-in-the-dark stars.

"It really bothers me that we haven't done anything ourselves yet," Kelsey went on. "Specifically targeting the cheerleaders, I mean."

"You're right," Mallory said. "We can't let the guys fight our battle. And we can't let the Spartan cheerleaders think they're getting away with what they did."

The run-in with the Lacede student council still occupied my mind. How could people I'd never met before have so much animosity toward me? I hadn't even had a chance to say something inadvertently insulting or rude to them. Just because I went to Troy, they automatically hated me?

And why did Greg just push me out of the restaurant like that? Was he choosing them over me?

A pillow landed on my face, startling me.

"Stop zoning out and start offering some advice," Elena said. "Any suggestions about what we can do to get the Spartan cheerleaders back?"

I sighed loudly. "I have no idea. Freeze their bras?"

"We're not in sixth grade," Mallory told me. "And how would we get access to their bras?"

"Fine," I snapped. "Don't ask me for help if you don't want to listen to me."

"What's wrong with you?" Kelsey asked, shooting an annoyed look in my direction.

"Nothing," I said.

Elena bounced onto the bed next to me, shaking me around. "Aw, come on, Cassie. You can tell us. We know something's bothering you."

"Did you get a bad grade on that algebra quiz?" Kelsey asked, patting my knee. "That's okay. I heard Ms. Jenkins always throws out the lowest quiz scores at the end of the semester."

"It's not algebra," I said. "It's boys. Or one boy in particular."

A squeal multiplied by three nearly shattered my eardrums.

"Tell us all about him," Mallory said. "Do we know him?"

"Well, um . . ." I wasn't too eager to tell Mallory and Kelsey that my boy problem was about a Spartan.

"You don't know him; it's a guy Cassie met a few summers ago," Elena said quickly, jumping to my rescue. She must have guessed who the boy was. "What's the problem?"

I rolled over and buried my face in the comforter. "What isn't the problem? I kissed him a month ago and he just hasn't said anything about it. He's been acting weird ever since then. I've pretty much taken the hint that he doesn't want to be anything more than friends, but couldn't he have the common courtesy to just be honest?" I sat up, punching one of Elena's teddy bears. "He makes me so mad. He's treating me like I'm nothing, like I don't deserve respect."

"Okay, first of all, stop punching my bears." Elena

snatched the teddy bear away from me. "Second, if he's acting like that, he's not worth your time."

Mallory and Kelsey nodded.

"She's right," Mallory said. "There are tons of other guys out there, and if this one doesn't know how to treat you right, find someone who does."

I let out a long sigh. "But what if I don't want someone else?"

"Then you have to decide how much this heartache is worth to you," Elena said. "If you don't like the way he's treating you, you have to stand up for yourself. Make him see you as someone who deserves respect and honesty. And then let him know exactly how you feel. Tell him that you're not happy being just friends and if he doesn't want more than that, you can't be his friend anymore."

"I'm afraid to lose him," I said softly. The thought of not having Greg around, not being able to tell him anything or spend hours playing video games with him, hurt deep inside. Yeah, I had a huge crush on him and wanted to kiss him, but most of all I wanted to keep our friendship.

"You have to take a chance sometimes for the person you love," Elena said. "Sometimes you just know that a huge risk is worth it."

Was that how she saw Perry? Was he the person who

she felt was worth the risk, worth all the trouble that she had caused, just to be with him?

For the first time, I saw Elena and Perry's relationship not as something that was done just to spite Lucas or to start a war between our schools, but as a connection between two people who truly wanted to be together. I almost felt, well, as if I respected Elena for taking the chance despite everything.

I smiled at her. "Thanks," I said.

She smiled back. "No problem. That's what friends are for."

Elena sat back, looking at the three of us. "Now," she said, "what are we going to do about those cheerleaders?"

16

"ARE YOU SURE YOU REALLY WANT ME HERE?"
I stood on Greg's front porch, my arms crossed over my
chest as if to keep Greg at a distance from me.

"Of course I want you here," Greg said, giving me a
confused look. "Why would I have called and invited you
over if I didn't want you here?"

I shrugged. "I don't know, but you couldn't seem to
get rid of me fast enough last weekend at TJ's. You know,
when all of your *other* friends showed up."

Okay, so I still felt mad about him choosing the
Spartans over me. I realized it was silly and that Greg had
every right to hang out with people other than me, but
still it hurt to be rejected and pushed aside like that. So

what if Greg already had an arranged meeting with those Spartans? He could have told them to get lost and spent the day with me.

Well, if he even wanted to spend the day with me.

"It was a student council meeting," Greg told me, running a hand through his dark hair. A big clump of hair stayed sticking up from the right side of his head. I had to fight hard to keep myself from reaching out and smoothing it down. "We had to discuss fund-raising ideas for this year. I wasn't trying to kick you out."

"Yes, you were," I said.

Greg sighed. "Fine. Yes, I wanted to kick you out before they got there. But only because I didn't want things to be uncomfortable for you. You know, one Trojan faced with a bunch of Spartans? I thought it would be better if they didn't see you so that they wouldn't have a chance to make any mean comments."

Why did he have to go and make it hard for me to be mad at him? Things would be so much simpler if I could just go on venting my anger and not feel ridiculous for getting upset over a stupid incident.

"Well," I said, raising my chin and trying to look as if I were doing Greg a favor by being in his presence, "I suppose I can forgive you then. Just this once."

"Thanks so much for the honor," Greg said, giving me

a lopsided grin. "Now, are you coming in or not? I've got the game all set up. And there's pizza."

"You should have said the word 'pizza' five minutes ago," I said, pushing past Greg as I stepped into the house. I followed the delicious cheese-and-tomato smell to the den, where the Martial Battle 2 Select a Character screen filled the TV screen and a large pizza with everything sat steaming on the coffee table.

"Extra mushrooms just for you," Greg said, handing me a plate as we sat down.

"You hate mushrooms," I reminded him.

Greg shrugged and took a big bite of his slice. "I'll deal with it."

For a long time, we ate pizza and played the game like we always did, laughing and taunting each other. It felt like everything that had happened in the last few weeks was just a dream. That I had never kissed Greg and messed things up. That our brothers weren't engaged in battle against each other. It was just Greg and me, like it had always been.

"You are dead meat," Greg said as his fighter lunged at mine on the screen.

"I don't think so," I told him, laughing as my fighter teleported out of reach.

We played four matches in a row and were tied when Lucas wandered into the room.

"I thought I smelled something in here," Lucas said, sneering at me.

Greg's expression grew stony. "Lucas, don't even start."

"Relax, little brother. I meant the pizza." But he sneered at me again before reaching over and stealing a slice.

"Ugh," Lucas said, settling down into the armchair and propping his feet up on the coffee table next to my can of soda. "Who put all these mushrooms on here?"

"Cassie likes them," Greg said.

"Oh, of course. I forgot. Anything *Cassie* wants. You know what I call that, little brother? Whipped. This *Trojan* has you wrapped around her little finger."

I glared at Lucas, but he ignored me as he stuffed half of the pizza slice in his mouth.

"If you're going to talk like that, you can go back to your room," Greg said. "No one invited you in here."

"Fine," Lucas said, rolling his eyes. "I'll keep my mouth shut so that I don't offend your *Trojan* girlfriend." Every time he said "Trojan," he emphasized the word like it was an insult.

I would never understand how Greg and Lucas could actually be brothers and share the same genes. But then, I didn't understand how I could possibly have the same genes as Perry and Hunter.

Lucas kept his word and stayed silent while Greg and

I continued to play. Greg's focus didn't seem to be entirely on the game anymore now that Lucas was in the room and so I easily beat him three times in a row.

At the end of the last match, when the game declared me the winner again, Greg stood up. "I need another soda," he said. "Cassie, you need anything?"

I shook my head. "I'm good."

"I'll take a Coke," Lucas said.

Greg scowled at his brother. "Get it yourself," he said before leaving the room.

As soon as Greg had disappeared, Lucas jumped up from the chair and lunged toward me. I thought for a moment that I might have to attempt some of the moves my dancing-lady character did in the game to fend him off, but thankfully, Lucas came to a stop in front of me. Then he dropped to his knees so that we were eye level with each other.

"Cassie," he said in strange voice, "I need you to help me with Elena."

I blinked at him. "Help you do what with Elena?"

"Win her back," he said.

Why did everyone think I was the expert on winning over Elena Argos? And what exactly was it that made both my brother and Lucas Mennon completely lose their minds over her? More important, how could I possibly get my hands on whatever it was that made boys go crazy so that I could use it on Greg?

"Sorry," I said, "but I think Elena has moved on."

Lucas grabbed my hands in his, moving so quickly I didn't have time to react. "Cassie, please. I don't know who else to talk to about this. Elena won't answer my calls or texts. I can't stop thinking about her. She means everything to me."

I pulled my hands from his grasp. "You probably should have told her that back when she was still with you. You two always fought. I never heard you say one nice word to each other."

"We did," Lucas protested. "You just didn't see it. Elena and I really loved each other."

He had completely gone off the deep end. "Lucas, get a grip," I said. "Elena has a new boyfriend. Move on."

Lucas's expression changed suddenly and he glared at me. "This whole thing is her fault." His voice rose and his neck turned red. "If she had just stayed with me instead of running off with some Trojan, our schools wouldn't be having this war. It's her fault, Cassie, and your brother's. And yours, too. I know you helped them get together. Don't you want this war to end? It'll all be over if you help me get Elena back—"

"What's going on?" Greg asked as he came back into

the room. He looked between Lucas and me, raising his eyebrows. "Cassie, you okay?"

"Of course she is," Lucas said, standing up and sounding like his usual self. "We were just having a chat."

Greg looked at me. "Cassie?"

I smiled and nodded. "Everything's fine. Lucas and I were just talking, like he said. I gave him tips on how to beat you in Martial Battle 2."

Greg didn't look like he believed us, but he didn't ask any more questions. Lucas let out a loud burp and said, "Well, I'm stuffed. I'm going to bed."

I watched Lucas leave the room, still not quite believing what had just happened. That was too weird. Lucas had never asked me to do anything for him before and now he wanted me to help him steal Elena back from my own brother?

Although . . . maybe it wouldn't be such a bad idea. If Elena and Lucas got back together, Lucas would forget this war on Perry and then everything could go back to normal. But would I be the worst sister ever if I even considered helping get Elena back with Lucas?

"It's getting dark," Greg said, glancing out the window at the darkening sky. "I'll ride to your house with you to make sure you get there okay."

"Who's going to make sure you get back home okay then?" I asked.

Greg puffed out his chest. "I can take care of myself."

"And I can't?" I asked. "What do you think I am, some defenseless little girl?"

"Sorry," Greg said, rolling his eyes. "I didn't mean to offend you. What I meant to say was, let me ride home with you so that I can protect innocent pedestrians from making the mistake of thinking that they could easily overpower a ninja disguised as a five-foot-tall, one-hundred-pound girl."

"Don't make me remind you that in the race for ultimate Martial Battle 2 champion, I am so kicking your butt," I said as I followed Greg outside to get our bikes.

It secretly thrilled me that Greg wanted to spend extra time with me by riding all the way to my house. Guys didn't do that for girls that they didn't like, right? And even though I knew Greg liked me only as a friend for now, I still hoped that maybe somewhere deep down inside there might be just a tiny spark of "romantic like" waiting to come out. Hopefully sometime before college, or else I might go completely insane trying to figure this romance thing out.

We raced each other back to my house, with Greg winning by two seconds. I scowled at the smug grin he gave me when we both had skidded to a stop in front of my house.

"Just a bike race," I said, panting a little. "I'm still beating you in the game."

Greg shrugged. "For now."

"Forever," I corrected him, reaching over to punch him lightly on the arm.

"You sure have an inflated sense of self-worth for someone so small," Greg told me.

This time the punch I gave him was a little harder and Greg held up his hands, laughing. "Okay, sorry! You—and your ego—are both perfectly proportioned."

"Thank you for noticing," I said, laughing also.

A shadow fell across us and I looked toward the house to see a big figure standing in front of the living-room window, looking out at us. Hunter.

A moment later, the front door opened and Hunter stared stone-faced across the yard. "Cassie, come inside," he said.

"I will when I'm ready," I told him.

"Two minutes," he said, tapping his watch for emphasis. He narrowed his eyes at Greg and then stepped back into the house, shutting the door behind him.

I groaned. "He is so annoying. He always thinks he can tell Perry and me what to do."

"You probably should go inside," Greg said, squeezing the brake handles on his bike and avoiding eye contact. "It's getting dark. And I should get home."

"Don't let Hunter run you off," I said. "You're my best friend and you have every right to be here."

Greg shook his head. "No, I don't. I'm a Spartan and this is Trojan territory. Do you really want people from your school looking out their windows and seeing you with me?"

I flailed my arms, frustrated. "I don't care what anyone else thinks! I'm not taking sides in this stupid fight."

"You are, Cassie," Greg said. He reached out to hold one of my hands and looked sad as he spoke. "We both are, whether we want to or not. I can't ask you not to be on your brothers' side, and you can't expect me not to do the same for mine."

"But this whole thing is ridiculous."

"I know. But it's not going to end, so we have to just go along with it and try not to let it tear us apart too much. I don't want to lose you."

My heartbeat pulsed throughout my entire body and echoed in my ears. My skin felt as if an electric current were running through it from where Greg's hand made contact with mine.

We weren't on different teams. We couldn't be. Greg and I had always been together, on the same side since the day we met. I wouldn't let Perry and Lucas mess everything up.

"I have to tell you something," I said in a voice so low I wasn't certain that Greg could even hear me. "The Trojans are planning to get the Spartan cheerleaders back for what they did to our locker room. Tomorrow before the game, when the cheerleaders are getting ready."

I knew I shouldn't have told Greg anything about the planned attack, but I couldn't stand the idea that we might possibly be enemies.

Greg looked surprised. He didn't say anything for a moment, then he whispered, "What are they planning?"

I shook my head. "I can't tell you that." I couldn't betray my brothers even more by revealing exact details. "I'm already going to be in huge trouble over this. Just do what you think is right with that little bit of information."

Greg squeezed my hand. "Okay. Thanks."

I tried to smile, but I felt terrible. I had proven myself a traitor to my school and my family.

The door to my house opened again and I almost felt relieved to see Hunter standing there again. "Time's up," he said, his voice all serious. "Come inside, Cassie."

"Bye," I said to Greg, pulling my hand reluctantly from his grasp and wheeling my bike toward the garage.

17

I DIDN'T TELL ANYONE WHAT HAD HAPPENED when I walked into the house. I ran straight up to my room and locked myself in for the rest of the night.

I knew I had to tell Elena that her plan had been ruined. But I didn't want her and the others to get mad at me when they found out. If Elena dumped me, I'd go back to being ignored and everyone would think I was a traitor to my school.

And Hunter would just say that he had warned me to stay away from Greg. This was my punishment for hanging around with Spartans.

I had to tell Elena. I just didn't know how.

All day at school on Friday, I kept opening my mouth, telling myself that this was it, this was the time to say something, and then . . . nothing came out. I couldn't force myself to say the words.

Time moved way too quickly and before I knew it, the end of the day had arrived and the final bell had rung.

I found Elena at her locker, thankfully alone. She wasn't likely to be alone for much longer though. I knew Perry or Mallory or Kelsey would soon come looking for her.

"Hey, Cassie," Elena greeted me, smiling wide. "We had a killer test in history today. I'm sure I failed."

"That's too bad," I said, trying to sound casual. "Hey, I really have to talk to you. Right now."

Elena closed her locker. "I'm meeting Perry out front. We're going over to my house to talk about you-know-what."

I knew what. The thing that I had ruined with my big mouth.

"That's what I came to talk to you about," I said. "Elena, you can't go to Lacede tonight."

Elena smiled at me. "Don't worry, Cassie. Everything's going to be fine. But you don't have to go with us if you don't want to."

"No, it's not that. The Spartans know that you're coming. You can't go."

Elena blinked at me, her smile gone. "How would they know?"

The question I had prayed she wouldn't ask me.

"That's not important," I said. "Just don't go to Lacede—"

"Cassie," Elena said, scowling at me. "How do the Spartans know what we're going to do tonight?"

She stared at me with a fierce look, like she knew already but wanted to hear me admit it. I had the sudden urge to run as fast as I could in the other direction.

But I forced myself to stay. I lifted my head and held my shoulders back, trying to look back at her without showing how crushed I was inside.

"I told them," I said.

Elena didn't flinch. She didn't change expressions at all.

"*You* told them," she repeated.

"I didn't mean to," I whispered. My voice suddenly wouldn't go louder than that. "It just came out. I'm so, so sorry."

Elena let out a long breath. "I'm sorry too," she said. "Bye, Cassie."

She turned around and headed toward the front doors without a look back at me.

This was it. Elena would tell everyone else what I had done and I would be an outcast at Troy once again. No, worse than an outcast. I would be so low that even the outcasts wouldn't come near me.

A few minutes after I arrived home, the door opened and Perry, Hunter, and Elena walked into the house. I sat alone in the living room, pretending to watch TV. My stomach dove into my feet when they came in, but I kept my eyes on the TV screen, trying to act as though I wasn't nervous about what they were going to say to me.

Perry and Elena sat down on the other end of the couch. Hunter stood in front of the TV, his arms crossed over his chest.

For several long moments, no one talked.

Finally, I said, "You're in the way of the TV." My voice came out squeaky.

Hunter didn't move. "Elena told us what you did," he said.

"Traitor," Perry muttered.

"I'm not a traitor," I said, looking away from Hunter to glare at Perry. I could deal with Perry being angry with me more than I could deal with Hunter being disappointed. "I didn't mean to tell them. It slipped out."

"What's done is done," Hunter said. "We're not going to Lacede tonight, so whatever the Spartans were planning to do to surprise us won't work."

I wanted to bury myself in the couch and never come out. "Is everyone mad at me?" I asked.

"No," Elena said.

I looked at her, surprised.

She shrugged. "We didn't tell them what you did. Only Hunter, Perry, and I know. We just made up an excuse about why we aren't going."

Relief flooded through me. "Thank you," I said.

Perry sneered. "Don't thank me. I wanted to tell them."

"Elena convinced us not to," Hunter told me. "She believes that you didn't mean to ruin the plan."

"I'm sorry."

Perry took the remote from my hand and started flipping through the channels. "You should be," he said. "Do you know how hard it is to find stink bombs around here? Now we've got a whole supply and no one to use them on."

"We'll plan something else," Hunter said. "For now, we have to call the other guys and try to figure out what the Spartans are planning."

"Count me out," Perry said. "Elena and I are going to her house to watch a movie and spend some time together." He reached over and ran his fingers through the ends of her hair.

Elena blushed, giggling a little.

"No, you're coming with me," Hunter snapped. "You can make out later."

"But—"

"End of discussion," Hunter said, shooting Perry a dark scowl. His face softened a little when he looked at me. "The plan tonight was ruined, but the Spartans haven't won yet."

I tried to smile. "Thanks for not telling everyone."

Hunter nodded slightly. "You'll still have to make up for this, but there's no reason everyone should know."

I wasn't sure I liked the sound of that.

18

GREG STOOD ON MY FRONT PORCH THE NEXT afternoon, his hands shoved into his pockets. He gave me his trademark lopsided smile. "Hey."

"Hey," I said, leaning against the open door as I looked at him.

"Can I come in?" he asked. "Or is this a Spartan-free zone?"

I stepped back, opening the door wider. "You can come in," I said. "Hunter and Perry aren't here right now."

Greg looked relieved as he walked past me. Mom stuck her head out of the kitchen to see who had been at the door. "Oh, hello, Greg," she said, smiling warmly at him.

"Hi, Mrs. Prince," he said.

"I haven't seen you in a while," Mom said. "We've missed you around here."

"Yeah," Greg said, his cheeks reddening a little. "I've been really busy with school and all."

Mom nodded. "Cassie's been really busy too. Well, I'll be in the kitchen if you two need me."

I led Greg into the den and we sat down on the couch. The TV was on and we stared at the screen for a moment in silence. I wasn't sure about Greg, but I couldn't pay attention to the TV at all even though I looked right at it. I kept focusing on the fact that Greg and I were alone, in my den, and he smelled so good. Soap and deodorant and his natural Greg smell. I wanted to lean into him and inhale his scent.

I cleared my throat. "So how are you doing?"

Geez, I sounded like we were casual acquaintances who hadn't seen each other in five years rather than best friends.

"All right," he said. After a moment of silence, he added, "The Trojans never showed up at the game last night."

I looked down at my lap. "That's good. Then there was no need for anyone to do anything."

"You told them, didn't you?" he asked. "You told them that you had told me about the plan."

I forced myself to lift my head and look him in the

eye. "I had to. It wouldn't have been right for me to let them go there without knowing the truth." I bit my lip. "Are you mad?"

Greg shook his head. "No. Lucas is. I knew you would tell the Trojans. But Lucas wanted to be prepared for them anyway. So we set up all kinds of traps around the locker rooms—you know, water balloons and buckets full of mud."

"I'll bet Lucas was mad that he went through all that trouble for nothing," I said.

"Well," Greg said, smiling a little, "we did get Coach Whittingham with the mud buckets, accidentally. It was pretty funny."

We laughed and I felt my body relax. This rivalry had both of us on edge and made things weird between us. I just wanted to go back to the times when we spent long afternoons together, playing video games and having fun.

I could feel Greg's gaze on me and I turned to look at him. He blushed, looking away quickly.

"What?" I asked.

"Nothing," Greg said.

He acted too weird for it to be "nothing." Usually when he came to my house, he would just plop himself down on the couch, put his feet up on the coffee table, and act like he was right at home. But this time he sat straight up on the couch, his feet on the floor and his hands on his knees. He looked like he didn't know what to do with himself.

"What's wrong with you?" I asked.

"Nothing," Greg repeated. "Why do you have to be so annoying, asking questions all the time?"

I grabbed a throw pillow and smacked Greg in the head with it. "How's that for annoying?" I asked.

Greg snatched the pillow out of my hands and pulled me toward him, wrapping one arm around my neck. With his free hand, he gave me a hard noogie right on the top of my head.

"Is that annoying enough for you?" he asked. "Because that's how much you're annoying me right now."

"Ow!" I cried. "Okay, okay, I give in. Stop!"

Greg stopped, releasing his grip on me. I lay with my head in his lap, looking up at him. His well-worn jeans felt soft against my cheek.

Greg lifted one of his hands and ran his fingers through the ends of my hair. I closed my eyes, wishing we could stay like this forever.

This was something that boyfriends and girlfriends did together, not two people who were just friends.

I sat up quickly, bumping my head into Greg's nose. Because for some reason, he had sort of slumped over, bending his head down toward me. Greg leaned back instantly, clasping his nose.

"I'm sorry!" I exclaimed. "Are you okay?"

Greg checked his hand for signs of blood, but thankfully there was none. "I'm fine," he said. "Just a little bump. What's gotten into you?"

My entire body felt hot. I suddenly felt like I was sweating in my thin T-shirt. "I just remembered something I need to do," I said quickly. I had to get Greg out of there before I gave into my insane impulses and kissed him. I would not make that mistake again.

"You have to go," I said, standing up.

Greg blinked up at me. "What?"

His lips were a soft shade of pink, his lower lip kind of pouty and—

"Out!" I shouted. "Go home right now."

"What has gotten into you?" Greg asked, wrinkling his forehead in confusion.

"Nothing. But you can't be here right now." I pulled Greg to his feet and pushed him toward the door.

But when I opened the front door, I found Elena and Perry standing on our front lawn, their faces attached at the lips. They broke apart when they heard the door open, and looked at us sheepishly.

"I'm not going outside while Elena and Perry are

out there," Greg told me as I pushed him onto the front porch.

"I don't care," I said. "Just go home right now."

My face felt hot, my heart pounded against my ribs, and my lips tingled as thoughts of kissing Greg flashed through my head. Maybe Elena knew what she was doing. Maybe kissing a boy, the right boy, really was worth all the trouble it could cause.

My hands pressed into his back and I pushed Greg farther into the yard.

Perry looked at us, smirking. "What's the Spartan doing here?" he asked.

"Nothing," I said. "Greg was just leaving."

"But Cassie—"

"Go!" I insisted.

Greg turned around to face me. "Do *not* make me walk out there in front of them," he said in a low voice.

"I'm sorry, but you really have to go before I do something I'll regret."

"Cassie—"

I stared at his collar to avoid looking at his soft, pink, oh-so-kissable lips. "Seriously, you have to leave now. Please don't ask questions, just go."

Greg looked at me for a moment longer, then shoved his hands into his pockets, turned and hurried toward the sidewalk without looking back at me or toward Elena and Perry.

Thankfully, Perry kept his mouth shut, mostly due to the fact that Elena used her lips to keep him from talking.

◆ ◆ ◆

"Cassie."

I rolled over, burying my head into my pillow.

"Cassie." The voice had grown slightly louder this time.

It hurt to open my eyes. I looked at the clock, blinking to bring the fuzzy numbers into focus: 2:53 A.M.

"Geez, Hunter, what is wrong with you?" I grumbled. "No one in their right mind is awake at this hour."

My brother stood hunched over my bed, dressed in a black hoodie and dark jeans. "Get up," he said.

"No way." I pulled the covers over my head.

Hunter snatched the covers away, dropping them on the floor. "Up. Now. Perry is waiting for us in the car."

I sat up. "What's going on? Are Mom and Dad okay?"

"Shh. Everything's fine," Hunter said. "We're going to Lacede."

I laughed. My brothers must have completely lost their minds.

"I'm going back to sleep," I said. "You two can do whatever you want."

I lay back down, but Hunter put his arms under my

body and lifted me from the mattress. "You have to go with us, Cassie," he said softly as he walked out of my room, carefully carrying me through the doorway.

"Put me down," I whispered as he headed toward the stairs. Visions of the two of us tumbling headfirst down the stairs flashed through my mind. "I can walk. If you'll let me get some shoes. And a jacket."

Hunter put me on my feet. "Fine, but hurry up. You don't have time to change."

I hurried back to my room, shoved my feet into the first pair of shoes I found, and pulled a jacket over my pajamas. Then I returned to the hall and followed Hunter down the darkened stairs.

"What is going on?" I asked as we headed outside. My brothers' car idled at the end of the driveway and Perry sat in the driver's seat.

Hunter opened the door for me, and I climbed into the backseat. Hunter sat down in front. Perry backed out of the driveway.

"I'll tell you when we get there," Hunter said. "Don't freak out."

I wanted to pound my brothers' heads in. "How can you tell me not to freak out when you won't even tell me what this is about? You wake me up in the middle of the night and say we're going to Lacede, but you won't say why. And I'm sure Mom and Dad have no idea that we're running around town right now, do they?"

"Relax, Cassie," Perry said. "None of us are getting any sleep until Hunter does what he's determined to do. So just sit back and enjoy the ride. It'll make things easier on all of us."

I sat back, crossing my arms over my chest and glaring at the backs of their heads. No one spoke as we drove across town. We stopped at the end of a driveway and a moment later, Elena joined me in the backseat.

"Hi, Cassie," she whispered. "I wasn't sure if you were coming."

"Why are you whispering?" I asked.

Elena giggled. "I have no idea, I just feel like I should."

I looked at my brothers, who both stared straight ahead into the night, and then leaned toward Elena. "What are we doing?"

She grinned. "You'll find out."

When we arrived at Lacede, two cars already waited there with a small group of people gathered around.

"There you are," Paul Baker said as we approached. He held a long, rolled tube toward Hunter. "Just got this from my brother tonight. It looks great." He grinned.

Hunter nodded. "Does everyone know what they're supposed to do?" he asked.

Everyone nodded, except me.

"I don't," I said. "I don't even know what I'm doing here."

"You all go ahead," Hunter said to the others. "I'll be there in a second."

When everyone except Perry and Elena had left, Hunter turned to me. "You're here because you have to decide what side you're on."

"I'm on neither," I said. "I'm neutral."

"You can't be neutral," Hunter said solemnly. "Friends or family, Cassie? Which will it be?"

I stared up at him, swallowing hard. How could he have me choose between him and Greg? This wasn't my fight.

"You can make up for ruining Friday night's plan," Perry told me. "Prove you're a real Trojan."

"What do I have to do?" I asked.

Hunter held the rolled tube toward me. "This is your night to play a prank against Lacede on behalf of Troy. Hang this banner somewhere that everyone can see it when they come to school tomorrow."

"That's it?" I asked. "Just hang some stupid banner and you'll stop questioning my loyalty?"

"That's it," Perry said with a smirk.

It would be a relief to get everyone off my back. "Okay," I said. "But from now on, you have to treat me like I'm one of you. Don't let everyone ignore me at school."

"Deal," Hunter agreed. "Elena will stay with you. Perry and I have business to attend to."

Perry sighed. "Can't I stay here with them? They might need someone watching out for them in case any Spartans come along."

"I doubt anyone else is coming by at three A.M.," Hunter said. "You're coming with me. You have to prove yourself in your own way, too, you know."

My stomach lurched. "What are you going to do?" I asked.

"Don't worry about that," Hunter said. He grabbed Perry's arm. "Come on."

My brothers disappeared around the side of the building, leaving Elena and me alone at the front.

"You'd better get to work," Elena said. "We don't have much time. Someone could come by and see us."

It wasn't too late to back out. I could go home and go back to bed and pretend this never happened.

"How are we going to hang this?" I asked, gesturing toward the banner Hunter had given me before he left.

Elena pointed to the front steps of the school. On either side were two brick walls that served as rails for the steps. "We can climb on them. Hunter put some nails and a hammer in his car."

They had already planned it all out. All I had to do was follow through.

"What does this banner say, anyway?" I asked, starting to unroll it.

"You can see after we hang it up," Elena said quickly. "It'll be a lot harder to manage it if you unroll it now."

I got the nails and hammer from my brothers' car and then followed Elena to the front steps of the school. She held the banner while I climbed onto the first brick wall. The wall was wide enough that I could stand comfortably, but I still felt a little nervous as I looked down at the ground below me.

I took the corner of the banner that Elena offered me and positioned it on the wall. Before I started hammering, I said, "We can get ourselves out of this, you and me. We'll go to the principal or whoever will listen and tell them everything that has been going on. We can—"

A cheer erupted from behind the school. I couldn't tell anything that was going on from my vantage point, but whatever it was my brothers had planned must have been successful.

"You can't do that to your own family," Elena told me. "Now just finish putting up the banner. The sooner you do, the sooner we can go home."

"Why are you a willing part of this?" I asked.

"Lucas made it personal," Elena said. "I can't back down now. I can't give him that satisfaction."

I turned back to the wall and tried to hammer the corner of the banner into place with as little noise as possible. Once I had the left side in, I jumped down and started climbing to the other side.

The rest of the group returned as I hammered the last nail in, carrying a large bag between them.

I eyed the bag. "What's that?"

"Nothing," Hunter said as Paul stuffed it into the trunk of his car.

"Nice," Mallory said, grinning appreciatively up at the banner I had hung. "It looks even better than I imagined."

I jumped down and stepped back to get a look. And then my jaw dropped open.

Hanging at least six feet wide before us was a blown-up picture of Greg. It was the picture from band camp that I'd stuck to my mirror. Greg's huge cheeks, stuffed full of grapes, grinned down at us. Written across the bottom of the banner, just in case anyone couldn't tell, were the words GREG MENNON: SOPHOMORE CLASS PRESIDENT.

I whirled around, facing the others. "Who stole my picture?" I demanded.

Elena turned away, looking at the ground.

I started toward the brick wall, intending to tear the banner down, but Hunter grabbed my arm.

"We have to go," he said, "before someone catches us here."

I tried to pull myself from his grasp, but he dug his fingers into my arm. "Come on, Cassie," Hunter said through clenched teeth. "We're leaving now."

My brother dragged me back to his car and pushed me into the backseat, ignoring my attempts to get away from him. As we drove away, I couldn't look at the banner that still hung, waving in the soft breeze.

19

MY BROTHERS AND I MADE IT BACK TO BED
without any problems. Mom and Dad were still fast asleep.

I felt exhausted when I got up for school the next
morning, but I dragged myself out of bed anyway.

I hadn't gotten much sleep after I made it back to my
bed because I'd been too busy worrying about what would
happen when Greg saw the picture I'd hung. Also, what
were my brothers doing last night? What if they had done
something really bad to the school?

But I couldn't tell anyone, not even Greg.

I waited all day for something to happen. Anything.
But nothing did. There was no evidence to even suggest
that we were the ones to blame. Ms. Fillmore didn't make
an announcement or hold an assembly. And my brothers

and Elena wouldn't reveal anything about what had really happened.

But that afternoon, I was sitting on my bed doing my homework when my bedroom door flew open. Greg marched into the room, his lips pressed into a straight line.

"*You* did this?" he asked.

I stared up at him, blinking. "What?"

"Don't try to play dumb with me, Cassie. You know exactly what I'm talking about. You're the only person who has that photo of me," Greg said.

"I—I—" I swallowed the lump in my throat and tried to speak again. "I didn't know that's what we were hanging, I swear. My brothers dragged me out in the middle of the night."

"So you just do whatever Hunter tells you?" Greg roared.

"He's my brother!" I shouted back, gripping my pencil tight in my hand. "And he thought I was a traitor to my school."

Greg glared at me, his nostrils flared. "So humiliating me in front of my entire school is how you save yourself?"

"I didn't want to do it. Elena stole the picture from me."

Greg's hands were clenched into fists. "You're not the Cassie I used to know."

I scowled. "What is *that* supposed to mean?"

"The Cassie I knew wouldn't have gone along with some stupid plan. The Cassie I knew would have come to me and apologized."

I stood up from my bed, letting my math book fall to the floor. "Hunter is my flesh and blood, no matter what he does, and you're just as mixed up in all this stuff as I am. And for the record, maybe you *don't* know me as well as you think."

Greg looked back at me with a mixture of anger and sadness on his face. "Maybe I don't," he said in a low voice. He turned toward my door and said, "Have a good life at Troy, Cassie."

And then he was gone, slamming my bedroom door behind him.

◆ ◆ ◆

That Friday, Troy played a home game against Forest High. Once again, I was in my uniform, sitting in the bleachers with the rest of the band.

Only five more games to go and then the football season would be over. I hoped that things would go back to normal after this. The other sports teams never seemed to be as influential as the football players.

I kept my attention on the field during the game. I had to admit that even though I wasn't into the school rivalry thing, it was still fun cheering for my brothers. They really were great athletes and I couldn't help holding my breath as I watched them on the field. Troy led the game 14–10, but Forest played well.

The buzzer sounded, signaling the end of the first half. The teams charged toward the lockers and people started getting up for refreshments. My mouth felt dry, so I headed over to the drink stand.

On my way to the refreshments, someone grabbed my arm. I turned around to see Mallory smiling at me.

"Wait a minute, Cassie," she said. "You won't regret it, I promise. The halftime show is going to be *very* interesting."

"Halftime show?" I asked. The only game that had a halftime show was homecoming, and that wasn't for a few more weeks. What was she talking about?

I didn't have to wait long for an answer. A figure dashed onto the field, jumping and leaping into the air. The Lacede High mascot. Someone dressed in the soft cloth body and giant head of the Lacede Spartan danced around the field, chased cheerleaders, and pretended to moon the spectators.

The crowd had stopped moving and watched the Spartan. Several people started to boo.

Why was the Lacede mascot at Troy? Was this something Lucas had come up with?

A movement at the other end of the field caught my eye. Several people dressed as Trojans ran across the grass toward the mascot, wielding fake swords and spears. They jumped on the mascot, tackling it to the ground and pretending to stab it with their weapons. One of the Trojans shoved a spear through the top of the mascot's head, high enough to avoid wounding the person inside.

The crowd cheered as the mascot pretended to die in a long, drawn-out, and overly dramatic death dance. The group of Trojans raised their weapons and chanted, "Troy! Troy! Troy!"

Ms. Fillmore marched across the field, followed by several teachers and coaches. The Trojans spotted them and took off in different directions, dropping their weapons on the grass. The once-dead Spartan came back to life and leaped to its feet, running as fast as it could in the costume.

Mallory grinned at me as the crowd around us laughed and cheered. "See? I knew you wouldn't want to miss it," she said before heading back toward the cheerleaders.

And then I knew what my brothers and everyone else had been up to the night we went to Lacede.

20

Dear Trojans,

As you are aware, Troy High School has had a long-standing rivalry with Lacede High School. In previous years, this rivalry has been good-natured, a fun additional burst of pep for both schools in our games against each other.

However, I am saddened by the actions of certain students this school year who have taken it upon themselves to turn this lighthearted rivalry into an excuse to damage school property.

Troy High School does not approve of the actions of these students. Last Friday night at our football game, a few students displayed their lack of respect toward our sister school by parading around our field in a stolen mascot costume.

Let me make this clear to all of you: Pranks such as these

will not be tolerated. The offending students involved in last Friday's prank have been caught and punished. If you have any further information on the events of the last few months, please feel free to see me in my office. My door is always open to you.

Let's please do what we can to mend things between Troy and Lacede. We are all neighbors and rely on each other in times of need. Rivalries are fun, but not at the cost of hurting others.

Thank you,

Miriam A. Fillmore, Principal

* * *

I skimmed over the letter that had been passed out during my fifth-period class on Monday and then crumpled it into a tight ball.

All day, no one had been able to talk about anything other than the mascot prank at the game. Three of the guys who had taken part had been caught, the one in the mascot costume and two of the Trojans. The other two had managed to get away and their friends had refused to give up their names, even though the would-be informants were given a week's suspension.

On the one hand, I was thankful to those guys who hadn't given up names. If they had, the trail may have eventually led to my part in hanging the banner.

But on the other hand, I wished everyone had been turned in and punished. Maybe that would have put a stop to this mess.

My brothers weren't in trouble, of course. They'd been playing in the game and had been in the locker room when the Trojans and Spartan mascot ran onto the field, so there was no way anyone could point a finger at them. Well, not without evidence anyway. All the students, it seemed, knew that Hunter and Perry had had at least some part in the theft of the costume.

But no one would turn them in.

They hadn't even denied it when some students talked about it during lunch. Hunter seemed indifferent to the attention, but Perry reveled in it. He probably hoped everyone thought it was all his brilliant idea.

Why didn't I just go tell someone what I knew? I knew everything—well, everything except how exactly the laxatives had gotten into the spaghetti sauce.

But Hunter and Perry were still my brothers and I just couldn't do that to them. Besides, if I did, I'd have absolutely no friends at all. The Trojans who had started to talk to me would certainly dump me as soon as word got out that I'd ratted out my own brothers. And with Greg no longer speaking to me, I would be entirely friendless.

The bell rang and I stood up from my desk along with everyone else and shoved my books back into my backpack. When I reached the door, I tossed my crumpled letter into the trash can.

Kelsey laughed from behind me. "I don't think Ms. Fillmore would be too pleased with your reaction to her very important words," she said.

I managed a small laugh. "You're not going to tell on me, are you?"

"Nope." Kelsey threw her own crumpled ball into the trash too. "Not as long as you don't tell on anyone." She eyed me for a moment.

"Who would I tell?" I asked.

Kelsey slung her backpack over one shoulder and gave me a huge grin. "Well, I'll see you later."

"Yeah," I muttered as Kelsey walked away.

◆ ◆ ◆

"What's going on?" Perry asked as our car approached Troy.

I looked up from the book I'd been reading in the backseat during the ride to school. People milled around the courtyard, both students and teachers. From our vantage point, we couldn't see what had their attention.

Hunter pulled into a parking space and the three of us jumped out of the car, hurrying toward the crowd.

"Hunter's here," I heard someone say. "He'll know what to do."

The crowd parted before us as more people noticed my brothers moving through it. I followed at Perry and Hunter's heels, getting more and more nervous about what exactly we would see.

When we reached the front of the crowd, I saw it. Students whispered and muttered to each other while teachers tried to break up the crowd and yelled at everyone to get to class.

But no one moved. I stood at the back of the group, staring up toward the statue of the Trojan—the statue that we proudly gathered around daily—seated on his horse in the courtyard.

Only now, instead of the slightly smirking head of the Trojan warrior, there was nothing. The Trojan was headless.

"The head is gone," a guy behind me said to his friends. "I got a closer look at it earlier, before the teachers started pushing us back, and the Trojan's head was cut completely off."

"All right, everyone!" Ms. Fillmore appeared, wielding a megaphone in front of her mouth. "Everyone get to class *now*!"

"Spartans suck!" someone shouted.

"We need to fight back!" someone else said.

A cheer arose from the students around me. Ms. Fillmore glared around at us and spoke into her megaphone again.

"Did you not hear me the first time? Anyone who does not go to class right this minute will be suspended. Go!"

The crowd started to break up and I let myself get caught up in the flow of bodies headed through the double doors of Troy High. Just inside the doors, people flocked toward Hunter.

"What do we do?" Paul Baker asked my brother. "We can't let the Spartans get away with this."

"They've gone too far," Perry said, nodding.

Hunter rounded on him. "And just what are you going to do about it? I've been the one who's had to make every decision throughout this entire thing! I'm bearing the burden of your little love triangle while you do nothing but kiss your girlfriend and then bask in my glory. As if you honestly had any part in it! The only thing you've had a part in, Perry, is making this rivalry an all-out war."

Perry's nostrils flared as he stared back at our brother. "Don't you try to blame all this on me. Lucas Mennon started this war just because he can't deal with the fact that his girlfriend didn't want him anymore. I didn't start this war, but if you're so sick of leading us to victory, I'll do it myself."

The students standing in a circle around my brothers

were completely silent, their gazes moving back and forth between Hunter and Perry. I spotted Elena on the other side of the circle across from me. Her face had paled and her eyes had grown huge.

Everyone probably expected my brothers to get into a fistfight right there in the hall. The tension rising between them certainly felt like someone was about to throw a punch.

But they didn't know Hunter as well as I did. Physical fights weren't his style, unless someone attacked him first. Hunter and Perry argued a lot, but Hunter preferred to fight with words and strategy rather than fists.

So I was probably the least surprised of everyone when Hunter took a step back and said, "No. I will settle this once and for all. Go sit with your girlfriend and look pretty, like you always do."

Hunter turned and walked away.

21

HUNTER AND PERRY'S FIGHT HAD SHAKEN ME more than I'd realized. All day it was the only thing I could think about. I didn't talk much to anyone and I snapped at Elena when she kept going on and on about how worried she'd been that Hunter was going to punch Perry in the nose.

When I got home that afternoon, I sat down at my computer and opened my e-mail.

No messages, other than spam. I didn't expect there would be. Greg was the only person who ever e-mailed me, and I seriously doubted that he would send me anything now.

I clicked on New Message and poised my fingers over the keyboard. After a few minutes, I started typing.

Dear Greg.

No, that was too formal.

Hey, Greg. It's Cassie.

Of course he knew it was me. He would know my e-mail address.

Just wanted to say I'm sorry about everything. I should never have gone to Lacede that night. But you shouldn't act so high and mighty. You're just as much to blame as anyone else—

Oh, yeah, that would really make things better between us. I started again.

Greg, I miss you.

The screen became fuzzy and my eyes burned with tears. I wiped them away, but more came in their place.

I lay on my bed later, still sobbing, when I heard my bedroom door open.

"Cassie?"

"Go away," I said, burying my face in my pillow.

I felt the mattress sink down under my brother's weight. A warm hand rubbed over my head.

"Cassie," Hunter said, "why are you crying?"

"I'm not," I said. "Now, go away."

But Hunter didn't make any movement. "I'm not going away until you tell me what's wrong," he said. "Do I have to play the big brother card and beat someone up for you?"

I rolled my eyes. "That's not your style."

Hunter let out a long sigh. "Yeah, but I've done a lot of things lately that aren't exactly my style."

I rolled over and looked at him. "Then why do them? Why can't you just end this?"

"I know you don't understand," Hunter said, reaching over to wipe tears from my cheek. "But I am doing this to make things better for you. Next year, I won't be at Troy anymore. If I back down, things between Troy and Lacede could get worse. I'm trying to end this rivalry once and for all so you won't have to deal with it after I'm gone."

"But things are worse now than they've ever been before," I said. "If you all will just stop this stupid fighting, we can get back to normal."

Hunter didn't say anything for a long time. Then finally he said, "I want it to end just as much as you do. But until one side proves that they are stronger, smarter, and better than the other, it will go on and on. I need to end this for you and Perry."

I turned around so that my back was to him. "Then go away and leave me alone."

"Cassie," Hunter said, sounding a little annoyed. "I know you're upset because of what happened between Perry and me this morning—"

I sat up suddenly, whipping around to face him. "Not everything is about you and Perry! If you two would stop being so . . . so pigheaded, you might notice that people have lives outside of you. Not *everyone* at school worships the ground you walk on. And some of us wish you all would go away and let us live our lives in peace because we were a hundred times happier before you started this fighting. Now, *get out!*"

I screamed the last words at my brother, startling him. I had never yelled at Hunter like that. He had always been the brother who looked out for me, who kept Perry from tormenting me, the one who carried me home crying in his arms when I fell off my bike.

But all I wanted now was for both of my brothers to disappear. I wanted all of this to end. My brothers had already cost me the best friend I'd ever had. Couldn't they leave me alone to cry in peace?

Hunter's jaw twitched, but he stood up and walked

toward the door. "I'm sorry, Cassie," he said. "I'm sorry you don't understand."

◆ ◆ ◆

"Come on, Cassie!"

I shielded my eyes from the sun with one hand and looked across the sand toward the blue-green water. Elena, Mallory, and Kelsey had waded knee deep and shrieked as the waves crashed toward them.

"Too cold!" I shouted in response to Elena's call. While they pranced around in bikini tops and shorts on the warm mid-October day, I stayed in my T-shirt and capris.

I hadn't wanted to go to the beach, but Elena had insisted that it was just the thing to cheer me up. I thought I'd been hiding my mood from everyone ever since my outburst at Hunter four days earlier. My brother hadn't spoken to me since then, and he hadn't even bothered to keep Perry from teasing me.

Not that Perry paid much attention to me lately, especially not if Elena was around. I looked toward where he and some of the other guys from the football team were throwing a football across the sand. Perry kept looking at Elena, checking her out while she played in the water with Mallory and Kelsey.

I wished I could see things as simply as Elena did and cheer myself up with a day of sun and sand. But I just didn't have the energy to put that much effort into pretending to be okay.

Looking away from the water, I spotted Hunter on the rock jetty he'd been sitting on for half an hour. At first, some of the other guys had gone out there to try to talk to him, but then they'd all come back to shore, leaving Hunter still sitting there alone.

A shadow fell over me and I turned back around as Elena sat down on the blanket.

"Are you just going to sit here all day feeling sorry for yourself?" she asked.

"I'm not feeling sorry for myself. I just don't want to get in the water."

Elena rolled her eyes. "You're moping, Cassie. What has gotten into you lately?"

I picked up a handful of sand and let the golden grains fall between my fingers. "Nothing. I just wish this stupid thing with Lacede would hurry up and end."

"Me too," Elena said. "It's all anyone can talk about."

"Thanks to you," I muttered.

"What?"

I scowled at her. "I've been blaming everything on my brothers, but it's really all your fault. You started this entire thing by dumping Lucas for Perry."

Elena looked stunned, as if I had slapped her. "If I

recall correctly, you helped me win over Perry. If you didn't want me going out with him, you should have said something two months ago!"

"Yeah, like it would have done any good. Girls like you always get whatever they want, no matter who gets hurt."

Elena's mouth fell open. She looked at me, her eyes glassy with tears. "I can't believe you would say that, Cassie. I thought we were friends."

"You used me to get close to my brother and you stole my picture of Greg from my room," I said. "We were never friends."

"That's not true," Elena snapped. "Well, okay, part of it is. I did steal the picture. I'm sorry, but I had to, just like you had to hang that banner to prove something to your brothers. But I never used you to get close to anyone. I liked you for *you*, because I thought you were nice and caring. Guess I was mistaken."

Elena leaped to her feet, but she didn't walk away just yet. "You know, Cassie," she said, "you're right about one thing. Girls like me do get whatever they want. You know why? Because I'm willing to go for it. You won't see me sitting around crying about how everything is so unfair and doing nothing to change it."

She spun around and marched back toward the water, kicking up sand behind her.

22

I WAS ENTIRELY, COMPLETELY, UTTERLY ALONE.

It was worse than it had ever been before. I should have been used to everyone ignoring me, but this time it felt terrible. I would walk through the halls like a ghost, no one even taking a second look at me. Elena made sure to stay busy talking to Perry or Kelsey or Mallory, and in English class she kept her eyes on her textbook and pretended she didn't see me.

This time, I didn't even have Greg to talk to outside of school.

And since homecoming was only a week away, things at Troy had become even crazier than they already were. Students cheered for the football players as they walked down the hall and people randomly yelled out, "Trojans!

Trojans!" to get everyone around them wound up. The former Lacede students who now attended Troy had to deal with constant harassment from a few of the Trojans. Kids were getting shoved sideways into the walls, tripped, and their books knocked out of their arms. No amount of discipline from the teachers would stop it.

On the following Friday night, I sat with the band at Cresswell High, where we were playing an away game. But although the other members of the band surrounded me, I had never felt more alone.

I tried to smile at the two fellow flautists sitting next to me, but I guess my smile came out looking weird because they just stared blankly at me for a moment. Then one turned to the other and said, loud enough for me to hear, "What's wrong with her?"

"She thinks she's something now that she's hanging out with cheerleaders and football players," the other girl said. "Just ignore her."

I had come full circle back to where I'd been three months ago. The popular crowd thought I was below them and the unpopular crowd thought I was too good for them.

The sound of music startled me from my thoughts and I dropped my flute on my toe. The Trojans had apparently scored a touchdown. Ms. Holloway stood in front of us, leading us through the music. She glared at me and motioned for me to pick my flute up. I did, but by the time I'd gotten it to my lips, the rest of the band had finished the song.

"Hunter is on fire tonight," someone behind me said. "Look at him fly across the field."

I found my brother among the uniformed guys and watched him for a few moments. He *was* on fire, playing like he never had before. He threw perfect passes and avoided being sacked. The entire team worked as one cohesive unit, moving elegantly through their plays. Troy managed to get nearly all the way down the field toward their end goal before Cresswell stopped them.

The guys lined up again and Hunter called out the play. The ball snapped and the guys swarmed across the field.

But something was wrong this time. The guy Hunter looked for wasn't where he should have been. Hunter held the ball back, his arm poised to throw, but he was unable to find anyone open to pass to.

Hunter didn't see the huge Cresswell linebacker headed toward him from the left. I wanted to call out to him, to warn him, but I was frozen in place, my flute gripped tightly in my hands.

Hunter threw the ball in the last second before the Cresswell player made impact with him. The ball tumbled through the air, heading toward no one. Hunter slammed into the ground under the linebacker's weight, falling hard on his right arm.

"Cassie! Sit down!" Ms. Holloway called to me as I pushed through the crowd toward the field. The referee had blown the whistle to stop the clock and a small crowd headed toward where Hunter lay on the grass.

I pushed myself to the front of the group of football players all standing in a circle around my brother. For a moment, I couldn't breathe as I looked at him. He lay so still, his eyes closed, his left hand gripping his right arm tight.

Just like in the dream I'd had a few weeks ago.

Coach Wellens kneeled and pulled the helmet from Hunter's head. "You okay, Prince?" he asked.

Hunter opened his eyes, and I let out a breath of relief. He was still alive. He didn't scream in pain and none of his limbs seemed to be stuck out at weird angles.

Everyone took a step back as Hunter sat up, still gripping his right arm to his chest. "I landed on my shoulder," he said.

The game medic took over and Hunter flinched only slightly as the medic turned his arm this way and that.

"Nothing's broken," the medic announced. "But you should let a doctor check you out."

"I'll call your parents," Coach Wellens said.

"No," Hunter told him. "I'll stay and watch the rest of the game."

Coach Wellens scowled. "Don't try to be a hero, Prince—"

"I want to stay," Hunter said. He looked up at the coach with a look in his eye that let us all know he wouldn't be persuaded to do otherwise.

"I'm still calling your parents," Coach Wellens said. "If they say it's okay, you can do whatever you want. Since you're going to anyway," he muttered.

Perry helped Hunter to his feet and the other players headed back to the sidelines to regroup before continuing the game. For a moment, I was the only one not moving, just watching my brothers as they walked side by side toward the Troy benches. The other guys on the team clapped Hunter on the back as he joined them, and the cheerleaders cheered. The spectators had applauded when Hunter stood. Even the Cresswell crowd joined in to offer him support.

I stood alone, in the middle of everything but part of nothing. No one would notice if I stood there all night—

"Miss, you'll need to get off the field."

I looked up into the eyes of the referee, who was motioning for me to get off the grass so they could restart the game.

◆ ◆ ◆

"How's Hunter?" I asked Mom the next day.

Mom dropped the two bags of groceries she had carried in from the car on the kitchen counter and sighed. "I just got off the phone with your dad," she told me. "They're still at the doctor's office, but the good news is that nothing is broken. It's just a mild sprain. The doctor says Hunter will need to take it easy for a few days, but he should heal up just fine."

"That's good," I said, stirring the vegetable soup in my bowl. Then I thought about something. "Our homecoming game is next Friday. Will Hunter get to play?"

"I don't know," Mom said as she put away the groceries. "I guess it depends on how easy he is on his arm over the next few days. We'll have to wait and see."

Without Hunter in the game, did we have a chance of winning against Lacede? It was the biggest game of the season, the Spartans versus the Trojans. There was no way Hunter would want to miss playing that night.

But maybe it would be for the best if he did miss out. A chill spread up my spine as I remembered my brother lying on the grass the night before, his eyes closed. His injury could have been worse. My dream about him lying there, pale and unmoving, still flashed through my mind.

Against Lacede, it was very likely that he could be hurt much worse.

"So," Mom said, "speaking of homecoming, are you excited about the dance?"

Ugh. Why did she have to remind me about the dance? I'd been trying to ignore it. I had no friends, no date, and no reason at all to go to the dance anymore.

"Not exactly," I answered. "I think I've decided I'm just going to stay home."

Mom turned away from the cabinet, a box of stuffing mix in one hand. "What? You can't stay home on *homecoming!*"

"Well, I'll go to the game," I said. "I have to since I'm in the band and we're doing this stupid halftime show. I still can't keep in step, you know. I'm going to make an idiot of myself. But anyway, once the game's over, I'll just ride home with you and Dad."

Mom put the box of stuffing in the cabinet and shut the door firmly before turning back to stare hard at me. "Cassandra Prince, you will do no such thing. You already made plans to go. Elena is expecting you to be there. You bought that great dress. And you can't let Greg down."

I couldn't look at my mom as I scooped up the last bit of vegetables in my bowl and said, "Greg isn't my date anymore."

Mom crossed the room in two huge steps and sat down next to me. "Oh, Cassie, what happened?"

I shook my head, blinking back tears. "Nothing. We're just not friends anymore."

"But you've been best friends for two years. How can you stop being friends for no reason?"

"Because he's a Spartan and I'm a Trojan," I said. "We should never have tried to be friends. Perry warned me after I came back from band camp two years ago that befriending a Spartan was asking for trouble." I snorted. "Guess he was right."

Mom put her hand over mine. "You don't really believe that. You and Greg shouldn't throw your friendship away just because of some silly pranks going on between your schools."

"It's not just silly pranks anymore," I said. "Maybe it was all fun and games when you were in school, but things are a lot more serious now."

Mom leaned back in her seat. "You think it was all fun and games when I was your age? Well, I attempted to pull a prank against the Spartan cheerleaders when I was a sophomore. But the cheerleaders somehow found out what I was up to and surprised me just as I was climbing into the tiny window of the girls' locker room. I fell eight feet, busted my lip, and broke my arm." She crossed her arms over her chest and gave me a smug look.

How did I not know this about my own mother?

"What happened?" I asked.

"Well, I healed just fine," Mom said. "But I was grounded for three months for sneaking out of the house and attempting to damage someone else's property. Which was totally unfair, because the only thing I had planned to do was fill the cheerleaders' lockers with shaving cream."

I managed a small laugh. "I can't believe my *mom* would do something like that."

"I had to," Mom said. "This one Spartan cheerleader had made out with my boyfriend at the beach the week before. So I had to do something." Mom laughed. "But it worked out in the end. Because then another football player helped me carry my books around while my arm was in a cast and he was a much better kisser."

My cheeks burned at the thought of my mom making out with a bunch of different guys. How was it possible that I was her daughter? I'd only kissed one boy in my entire life, and that turned out to be a disaster.

"Mom," I said, "what made you think this guy was worth fighting for?"

Mom's forehead creased as she thought for a moment. "I don't know. I don't think I ever really thought it all the way through in those terms. I just knew that I couldn't sit idly by and let people walk all over me. There are things you have to fight for in life, Cassie. It's up to you to decide what's worth it."

Elena should have been my mother's daughter. They had so much more in common.

Mom ran a hand over my head, smoothing down my hair. "I don't know what's happened between you and Greg, but I have to tell you that from my point of view, what you two have is worth fighting for. Don't give up so easily on him, Cassie."

I tried to smile as Mom stood. "Thanks," I said, staring into the remains of my lunch.

23

GREG'S EYES WIDENED A BIT WHEN HE OPENED the door to see me standing on his front porch.

I looked down at my sneakers for a moment, then back up at him. "Hey," I said.

"Hey," he answered.

Part of me wanted to run away as fast as I could and pretend I'd never come over.

But the other part missed him like crazy.

Mom and Elena were right: I couldn't give Greg up without a fight.

So I took a deep breath and said, "Look, Greg, I'm really sorry about everything—"

But just as I started talking, Greg also said, "I shouldn't have said all those things to you—"

We stopped and looked at each other.

Then we laughed.

Greg stepped back, opening the door wider. "Do you want to come in?"

My legs felt trembly as I walked into Greg's house, but I wasn't sure why. I'd been inside his house hundreds of times. The house was quiet, except for the sound of the TV in the living room.

"Where is everyone?" I asked.

"Mom and Dad went out to pick up dinner and Lucas is with Owen and Ackley." He smiled. "It's just you and me."

His words sent a shiver throughout my body. I squeezed my hands together to stop them from shaking as I followed him into the living room. We sat, and I made sure to keep enough distance between us that I wouldn't be tempted to do anything crazy. Like run my fingers through his messy hair. Or throw myself at him and kiss his perfectly pink lips.

What was wrong with me? I wanted to attack my best friend and smother him with my mouth. I needed to be committed.

Okay, deep breaths. I could stay calm and collected and not go psycho around Greg. I wanted to keep his friendship, not drive him away forever.

"I'm really glad you came over," Greg said.

"You are?" My voice sounded low and raspy. I cleared my throat.

Greg nodded. "I wanted to come see you or call you or something. But I just couldn't do it. I thought maybe the banner prank was your way of letting me know you never wanted to see me again."

"Of course not," I told him. "I've missed you. I mean, I missed hanging out with you."

Greg smiled at me. "I missed you, too. I've had to put up with Lucas's cheating at video games. It's really getting annoying."

I laughed. "Poor you. Turn the game on and let's solve that problem with you getting a nice, honest butt-kicking."

"We'll see who gets their butt kicked," Greg said as he got up to plug in the game console.

We played for a long time without speaking. I had never been more thankful for video games. It gave me something to put my focus on and took my mind off the fact that Greg had moved a little closer to me on the couch when he'd sat back down.

Well, it took my mind off of it a little. But I was still overly conscious of every movement Greg made, especially when it caused the side of his leg to bump mine.

"So," I said, when I felt like my head would explode if I sat quiet any longer, "I really am sorry about yelling at you."

"Me too," Greg said. "I mean, I'm sorry for what I said. It was wrong of me to expect you to betray your brothers."

I became distracted by Greg's closeness again and it allowed his fighter to take down my dancing lady with a well-aimed kick to the head.

"How did we get so wrapped up in this war?" I asked.

"In my case," Greg said, "I'm kind of stuck in it by default. Lucas needs someone to watch out for him and make sure he doesn't do anything crazy."

"You mean crazier than releasing chickens in my school?" I asked.

Greg laughed. "Well, that was one of my crazier ideas," he admitted. "But Ackley would have talked Lucas into doing something much worse if I wasn't around."

"It's so stupid," I said, stabbing at the buttons on my controller with my thumbs. "If everyone would just get to know each other and put aside this rivalry, they might be friends. Lucas and Perry actually seem like they have a lot in common."

"Like the fact that they both enjoy making out with Elena Argos?" Greg asked, smirking.

I couldn't help laughing. "Well, there's that. I guess they could bond over kissing techniques."

It felt really good to laugh. Especially with Greg. This war between our schools had lasted way too long. I wanted everything to go back to normal so Greg and I could hang out like we used to.

"You know," I said, "the Trojans and Spartans getting to know each other isn't a bad idea."

"How do you expect to do that? Have a big picnic where we can all sit around and talk and eat peanut butter sandwiches?"

"No," I said. "But you being at homecoming with me is a step in the right direction."

Greg raised his eyebrows. "You still want me to go to homecoming with you?"

My hands started to shake again and I gripped my controller tighter. "Yes. I mean, if you want to. I already have the dress, I might as well wear it."

Greg cleared his throat. "Okay. I'll go."

"Really?" I asked. "You don't have to."

"I want to," Greg said.

"Thanks."

He smiled. "I'll be at the game anyway, to cheer on Lucas and the others. So it won't be any problem to stick around after for the dance."

How romantic. A date of convenience. Just what every girl dreamed of.

But I forced myself to smile. "Great," I said, trying to sound cheery. "Then it's a date."

"Yep," Greg answered.

And then my mind went completely blank. I couldn't think of a single thing to say, like I had lost all knowledge of the English language.

Greg didn't help matters. He just stared at the TV while our fighters battled.

I was almost thankful when I heard the front door open. At last, someone could say something to fill the awkward silence.

But my thanks disappeared when I saw Lucas walk into the room with Owen and Ackley.

"I thought I smelled the stench of a Trojan," Lucas said, sneering at me.

"Lay off her," Greg told his brother, not taking his eyes off the screen.

"Relax," Lucas said. "I'm not here to terrorize your girlfriend. I just want to ask her some questions. Is it true about your brother?"

My mind reeled from Lucas calling me Greg's girlfriend, so I almost didn't hear what he'd said after that.

"Is what true?" I asked.

"We heard Hunter broke his arm during the Cresswell game," Owen told me. He leaned against the door frame, his arms crossed. "Is he playing in the game Friday night?"

"It's just a sprain," I said, "not a broken arm."

"But he's out of the game, right?" Ackley asked.

I shrugged. "Don't know. We'll have to wait and see how his arm feels on Friday."

Ackley looked almost rabid with excitement as he cracked his knuckles and curled one side of his lip into a sneer. "If the Trojan prince is too weak to play, it will be even easier to take the Trojans down once and for all."

Greg scowled at them. "Not now, please?"

"Whatever," Lucas grumbled. "Tell the traitor I said hi, Cassie."

I rolled my eyes as they left the room. "Is he ever going to get over Elena?"

"She did break his heart," Greg said.

"I'm not forgiving what she did to him," I said, "but he's blaming this entire war on her."

"Well," Greg said, shrugging, "it is kind of her fault."

"It's his too!"

"I know," Greg said. "But maybe if she hadn't broken up with Lucas, things wouldn't be as bad as they are now."

I sighed. Of course Greg would side with his brother, even if his brother was a complete idiot. "Let's just forget it, okay? I don't want to talk any more about Trojans or Spartans for the rest of the night."

"Deal," Greg said, pressing the Start button on his controller to restart our game.

24

"LADIES AND GENTLEMEN," SAID THE VOICE through the loudspeaker system. "Welcome to the Troy High homecoming game!"

The crowd erupted into cheers. I had never seen the bleachers as packed as they were then. People sat shoulder to shoulder, and the sound of all the voices vibrated through the bleachers under me.

Everyone had come out to see the battle between Troy and Lacede. A sea of red and black filled Troy's bleachers, while the visitors on the opposite side of the field wore Lacede blue and white.

"And now," the announcer said, "please welcome to the field your Troy High School football team. *Trooooooooojaaaaaaaaaans!*"

The cheerleaders stood in two lines, their red-and-black pompoms up in the air. The football team ran between them, waving their helmets at the roaring crowd. Hunter, who had insisted his shoulder had healed enough for him to play, jogged at the head of the line. He seemed more reserved than the rest of the guys, his helmet tucked under one arm and his eyes staring straight ahead as he moved onto the field.

The Lacede team ran onto the field a moment later and the boos coming from the Trojan bleachers drowned out the visitors side's cheering. I sat with the rest of the band, my flute resting in my lap and the sounds from the audience around me thundering in my ears.

I could only focus half of my mind on the upcoming game. The other half obsessively thought about how much time remained until the dance. I had seen Greg earlier, but we didn't have time to talk because I had to stay with the rest of the band. As he passed, he just gave me a quick wave.

But that was enough to send my entire body shivering.

I couldn't do this. I couldn't go to a dance with Greg and pretend that we were just two friends hanging out. Hanging out meant playing video games in his den. It did not mean wearing a dress with spaghetti straps and putting on heels that pinched my feet.

A cheer from the crowd snapped me back to the game. Troy had opened with the kickoff, and the offensive line tried to force their way down the field. Patrick Hanson brought down a Trojan after only a few feet. The crowd booed around me.

I looked across the field at the Spartan sidelines. Ackley stood there, watching the game. He cheered when his friend Patrick tackled the Trojan, but then he just crossed his arms over his chest and stared stonily at the field again.

Why wasn't Ackley playing? He was Lacede's star linebacker. I'd seen him play enough times to know he was good. He had more tackles and sacks to his name than any of the other players. And it seemed like he'd want to be out there, trying to get revenge on Hunter for injuring him last year.

The play resumed and Patrick headed toward Hunter. But my brother passed the ball to another Trojan before Patrick could sack him. Patrick still tried to grab Hunter around the waist and bring him down, but Hunter swung himself around, flinging Patrick to the ground behind him.

It didn't stop there. Patrick went after Hunter every chance he got. Hunter soon learned to expect him. I knew my brother tried to go easy on him at first, since Patrick was much smaller, but after a while Hunter got more aggressive. My brother usually remained even-tempered during a game, but even he had a limit.

"And at the end of the first quarter, the score is seven-seven," said the announcer. "Great game so far by both teams. Can the Trojans pull ahead in the second quarter? We're about to find out."

As the guys returned to the field after a brief huddle, I hoped Patrick would leave Hunter alone. But no such luck. Wherever Hunter was, there Patrick went. Hunter tried to fake him out a few times, but Patrick easily changed his course to follow Hunter. He distracted Hunter so much that my brother fumbled the ball, something he rarely did.

I breathed a sigh of relief when the Spartans gained control of the ball again so Hunter and Patrick could go to their respective sidelines and cool off.

But my relief didn't last long. The Trojans quickly regained control of the ball and Hunter jumped right back onto the field. Patrick joined him.

My hands gripped my flute so tightly that the keys dug into my flesh. Something bad would happen if Patrick didn't back off, I could feel it. The dream I'd had about Hunter being injured flashed into my mind.

With only a minute and nine seconds left in the first half, something happened. Patrick charged at Hunter, his head bent. Hunter, instead of trying to avoid him, turned directly toward Patrick. The collision seemed to happen in slow motion.

Hunter tucked in his arms and head, driving his shoulder into Patrick's chest. Patrick wrapped his arms around my brother, almost as if trying to hug him. But then Hunter straightened up, pulling Patrick up over his back and sending him crashing to the ground behind him with a sickening thud.

Patrick lay on the ground, his arms and legs splayed out to his sides. He didn't move. Hunter stared down at him a moment, then stepped back as the Spartan coach and medic came running to Patrick's side.

"Number twenty-three on the Spartan team is down at the thirty-yard line," the announcer said, his voice echoing over the quiet audience. "Time on the clock has stopped."

Hunter watched from a few feet away as the medic removed Patrick's helmet and talked to him. Even from my distance, I could tell that my brother looked lost. He removed his helmet and tilted his head back to stare up at the floodlights around the field as he rubbed a hand over his face. What was going through his mind? Was he sorry for what he'd done?

Ackley rushed onto the field and knelt on the grass, leaning over Patrick. Patrick still lay there, staring up at the darkening sky and making no movement to get up. Around me, people murmured to each other.

"Is he okay?" someone asked.

"Serves him right," someone else answered. "That's what he gets for going after Hunter."

The medic on the field lifted one arm and motioned toward his assistants on the sidelines. The two young men rushed onto the field, carrying a stretcher between them. They wrapped Patrick's head and neck with a brace and then carefully moved him onto the stretcher.

"I am told that number twenty-three, Patrick Hanson, has suffered a hard blow to the head," the announcer said as the medics carried Patrick off the field. Ackley walked beside the stretcher. Even through his padding, Ackley looked ready to pounce. "Hanson is being taken to the hospital for an examination and will be replaced by Lacede High's number sixteen. . . ."

The game continued, although no one made much progress in the final seconds of the quarter. At the buzzer, the score was 17–10 with Troy leading.

I made my way down through the crowd. I had to be on the field for the halftime show in two minutes, but first I wanted to talk to Hunter. But by the time I pushed through the throng of people, he had already disappeared into the locker room, the door closing heavily behind him.

Patrick would be fine, I assured myself. Accidents like that happened during football games all the time.

Greg stood nearby and I started walking in his direction. But just as I reached him, Ackley met us with Lucas and Owen following.

Lucas scowled at me. "Go away," he said. "This is Spartan business."

I looked at Greg, but he just shrugged and gave me a reassuring smile. The guys turned and walked away, their heads bent together in conversation.

"What's going on?" Elena asked as she ran up next to me. She looked toward the guys' retreating backs. "They planning another stupid prank?"

I shrugged. "I have no idea. I'm not a Spartan."

Elena grinned. "Thank goodness for that. I can tell you it's not as great as those guys make it out to be."

I looked at her kindly. "Aren't you supposed to be mad at me?"

"Do you want me to be mad at you?" Elena asked, rolling her eyes.

"I'm really sorry I snapped, Elena," I said. "It wasn't fair for me to blame it all on you."

"It takes too much energy to be mad at people. And besides, you need someone to help you get ready after the game. I'll bet you have no idea what to do with eyeliner, do you?"

I held up my hands in a protective stance. "I'm not letting you anywhere near my eyes with anything pointy."

Elena laughed. "Aw, come on, Cassie. I promise not to blind you."

A whistle sounded and Ms. Holloway called out for all the band members to line up. "Gotta go," I said, waving my flute at Elena as I hurried away.

A light, misty rain drizzled down as I took my place with the rest of the band. I didn't look forward to the homecoming halftime show, mostly because I still couldn't keep in step the entire time. My knees trembled as I waited for the show to begin.

I stumbled a bit, but somehow I made it through the routine without causing any catastrophes. We moved around to spell out T-R-O-Y and then W-I-N on the field as we played the school song.

Once the band had retreated to the sidelines, the small parade that the school held every year circled the track that surrounds the football field. The homecoming king and queen rode out in a red convertible, waving to the crowd as the lights glinted off their aluminum crowns. Then the cheerleaders followed, doing cartwheels and shaking their pom-poms.

But the last parade float really caught my attention. Slowly moving along the track, pulled by a couple of golf carts, was a Trojan warrior and horse. The float had to be at least seven feet tall from the top of the Trojan's head to the bottom of the horse's feet. What looked like black flowers made up the Trojan's body, while red flowers made up the horse. A banner draped across the Trojan's chest read TROY HIGH.

Our principal, Ms. Fillmore, rode on the float along with the Trojan and horse. And next to her stood a man I didn't recognize, but he and Ms. Fillmore each had an arm slung around the other as they waved to the crowd. Ms. Fillmore wore a red-and-black Troy sweatshirt while the man next to her wore a blue-and-white Lacede jersey.

The horse slowed to a stop in front of the bleachers where the Trojan supporters sat, and Ms. Fillmore gestured to someone on the sidelines. Someone handed her a megaphone so she could address the crowd.

"Hello, Trojans!" Ms. Fillmore shouted. The crowd roared for a moment, until she held up her hand for quiet.

"Thank you so much for coming to this year's homecoming game and showing your support for our boys," she said. "Hopefully you'll all bring us good luck so we can win this game!"

The crowd cheered again, stomping their feet and letting out whoops of "Troy! Troy! Troy!" in pounding unison. It took several moments before Ms. Fillmore could continue.

"I would like to introduce my special guest for this evening," she said, gesturing to the man at her side. "Mr. Richard Yancey, principal of Lacede High School."

Mr. Yancey waved and nodded good-naturedly as the crowd let out a mix of applause and boos.

"Troy and Lacede have a long history together," Ms. Fillmore said, "but we are still, in the end, friends and neighbors. Mr. Yancey has a few words he'd like to say on behalf of Lacede."

Mr. Yancey took the megaphone and smiled wide at the crowd. His face shone under the floodlights and he held up two fingers to make the peace sign at us, making him look like a hopelessly unhip politician. "Thank you, Ms. Fillmore. And thank you all for letting me be here. We've had an eventful season, but I hope that none of you hold hard feelings against us Spartans. As Ms. Fillmore said, we are neighbors and friends. I know some things have been said and done between our two schools, but I am here on behalf of Lacede to extend the offer of peace."

The boos continued.

"A few weeks ago, I asked the Lacede High student council to work on a project that we could offer all of you," Mr. Yancey continued. "I don't expect it will make up for the damage done to your beloved Trojan statue, but I hope the gesture might begin the healing process between our schools. And so, Ms. Fillmore and Trojans," he said, gesturing toward the Trojan and horse, "please accept this beautiful float with our apologies. We hope that by the time the flowers have faded, your statue will be as good as new and wounds will be mended."

About half the crowd managed a smattering of applause, but as I looked around I noticed most people rolled their eyes toward one another.

"A stupid horse made of flowers doesn't make up for Lacede's pranks," someone behind me growled.

The gesture might have been nice in the eyes of Ms. Fillmore and Mr. Yancey, but it obviously didn't make a difference among the students.

"Thank you, Mr. Yancey," Ms. Fillmore said, having taken the megaphone back. "The float will be moved into the gym so that we can all enjoy it during the dance tonight and remember our friends at Lacede. Now, let's play some football!"

25

"GO, TROJANS!" THE CHEERLEADERS DOVE INTO a series of flips and cartwheels along the sidelines as the Trojan defensive line charged down the field toward the Spartans.

Perry managed to bring down Lucas, but not before Lucas passed the ball to Owen. A Trojan intercepted the throw and gained a few yards before being tackled to the grass.

On the sidelines, Hunter paced back and forth. Since Patrick had been taken out of the game, Ackley had taken over stalking him. He was focused only on Hunter. His threats about taking down Hunter and getting revenge for his injury last year repeated themselves over and over in my head. I shuddered as I remembered the fire I had seen in Ackley's eyes when he thought Hunter would be too injured from last week's fall to play tonight.

"Go, Perry!" a girl near me shouted. She and her friends cheered, pumping their fists in the air.

On the field, after Lacede had called a time-out, Lucas slammed hard into Perry as they passed each other.

Perry turned toward the ref, pointing an accusing finger at Lucas.

"Sorry, accident," Lucas said, loud enough for his voice to float toward the bleachers. He had taken his helmet off and plastered an innocent look on his face.

The referee gestured for both Perry and Lucas to go to their respective sidelines. When the referee turned his back, Lucas sneered at my brother before heading away.

I turned to the sidelines, where I saw Elena watching with fear.

Hunter and the offensive line headed back onto the field. As did Ackley and the Spartan defense.

The sun had set, and only the floodlights around the field illuminated the players. The grass glistened with water from the light rain that had fallen during halftime, and the guys seemed to glow as the light reflected off their helmets.

Hunter's lips moved as he shouted out plays to his teammates, but the roar of the crowd made it impossible for me to hear anything he said from where I was sitting in the bleachers. He snapped the ball, and the players went into motion. The guards blocked Ackley long enough for Hunter to make the pass, but then Ackley broke through, still intent on charging at my brother.

Hunter didn't back down. He met Ackley head-on, and the two tumbled to the grass, arms swinging and legs kicking. Neither of them seemed to realize that another Trojan had caught Hunter's pass and moved the team sixteen yards closer to the end zone before being tackled. The referee ran toward them, his whistle screeching.

"Personal foul, number fourteen, Lacede," the referee shouted, giving Ackley a penalty.

The play resumed and again, Ackley went after Hunter. He was more careful this time, doing whatever he could to keep from getting another penalty but still attack Hunter.

The Spartans came alive now that Ackley was on the field. They stopped the Trojans from advancing and intercepted passes at every opportunity.

On the next play, Ackley lunged at Hunter, causing him to throw a wild pass. Lacede intercepted and regained control of the ball. The Spartan offensive line returned to the field, working as if they all had one mind. The guards brought down any Trojans who tried to reach Lucas or anyone else in possession of the ball. Owen managed an impressive thirty-yard run, scoring a touchdown.

At the end of the third quarter, the teams were tied 17–17.

Hunter didn't sit down to rest whenever he was off the field. He paced along the sidelines and kept his hands balled into fists at his sides. Some of the other guys tried to talk to him, but I knew he probably didn't even hear them. Ackley was tormenting him, and I knew Hunter was focused on nothing else.

The final minutes of the game ticked down. Lacede had managed to pull ahead, 24–17. The guys on both teams looked visibly tired, but the Trojans huddled one last time, trying to rally themselves. The other guys slapped Hunter on the back and shouted encouragements, but Hunter seemed as if he barely noticed his teammates' existence. He kept his head turned toward where Ackley stood across the field from him. And Ackley did the same, watching my brother's every movement.

"Come on," I whispered, glancing at the game clock. "Let's get this over with."

The sooner the game ended, the happier I would be. Maybe once Lacede and Troy had fought here on the football field, we could move on from this stupid rivalry for a little while.

With six seconds left on the clock, the Trojans lined up to attempt the last few yards for a touchdown. The center snapped the ball and both teams lunged forward.

Ackley, of course, charged at Hunter. One of the Trojan guards reached out to grab Ackley to stop him from hitting Hunter, but Ackley leaped over the guard's hands and continued on.

Ackley caught Hunter by surprise and he was unable to make the pass. Hunter had no time to hunch down and prepare for the impact.

Ackley wrapped his arms around Hunter as he tackled him roughly, turning Hunter so he landed on his right side. Hunter's feet flew out from underneath him first and he landed hard on his shoulder in the grass. The ball fell from his hand and rolled a couple of feet away.

The clock buzzed as it hit zero.

The bleachers were silent.

The coaches and medics for both teams rushed onto the field. People around me stood so they could get a better look at what had happened. But for a long moment, I couldn't do anything other than sit exactly where I was, my flute clutched tightly in both hands and my heartbeat throbbing in my ears.

Then something inside me snapped.

Ms. Holloway tried to stop me as I raced down the

bleachers, almost kicking several people in the head as I scrambled over them. "Cassie, stay here!" she shouted, reaching for my arm.

I had learned a thing or two from playing football with my brothers in the backyard, and I easily dodged out of her reach. I practically leaped over the people on the bottom bench as I hurried toward my brother.

Please let this be like last time, I thought. *Just a mild sprain.*

But as I pushed my way through the small crowd gathered around, I knew this wasn't like last time. Because as I drew closer, what I had seen in my dream weeks ago played itself out on the grass in front of me.

I skidded to a stop, staring horrified at my brother as he lay so still.

Ackley pushed himself up and stepped back, limping slightly on the ankle Hunter had injured last year. He pulled off his helmet and watched as the medic pushed at Hunter's shoulder, a sneer on his face. "The Trojan prince has fallen," Ackley shouted.

As Ackley turned around, his gaze met mine. His big eyes were wild. A large welt grew on one cheek and a little bit of blood trickled from his lip. I shuddered as he stared back at me. He looked so frightening; I had to look away.

Hunter grimaced. He bit his lip to keep from crying

out as the medic pushed on his right shoulder with his fingertips. I started toward him, but a hand grabbed my arm. Perry.

"Let them do their work," Perry said. "Hunter will be fine."

I shook my head as Hunter grunted in front of us. "He's hurt," I said. "What if he . . ."

I had started to say "What if he can never play football again?" but I couldn't even get the words out. Hunter without football was impossible to imagine. It had been his life since Dad had bought him his first football when he was six. For as long as I could remember, Hunter lived and breathed football. And he was counting on a scholarship for college.

The panicked, frightened feeling from my dream overwhelmed me. This wasn't just another injury; I knew in my gut that something was terribly wrong. I squeezed my eyes shut as Hunter let out a low moan.

"Let us through!" said a familiar voice behind me. "That's our son."

Mom pushed through the crowd first, followed by Dad. They dropped to their knees at Hunter's side. Mom leaned over him, smoothing back his hair and kissing his hand.

"He's landed hard on his right shoulder," the medic said. "He needs to see a doctor."

Behind us, the crowd in the bleachers murmured as they watched. For the second time that night, the medics carried a stretcher onto the field. They carefully rolled Hunter onto it, but I noticed the intense look of pain on his face.

I started after the stretcher as the two medics carried Hunter away, but Mom turned around and stopped me. "No, Cassie. It's okay. He'll be all right. You stay here and enjoy the dance."

"You expect me to *dance* at a time like this?" I asked, waving my flute around.

Mom patted my cheek. "There's nothing you can do for him. We're taking him to the hospital, and I'll call you later to let you know how he is. Okay? You have a big night ahead."

I knew Mom was right. I wouldn't be of much use at the hospital.

"Call me as *soon* as you know anything," I said.

Mom nodded, blew a kiss to Perry and me, and then hurried after Dad and Hunter.

"He'll be okay," Perry said, squeezing my hand. I knew he was trying to sound strong for me, but I could hear a waver in his voice. "He has to be."

26

"STOP BLINKING!" ELENA GRABBED MY CHIN IN one hand, digging her fingertips into my flesh.

"Stop trying to tear my eyelids off!" I snapped.

"It's just a little bit of eye shadow," Elena said. "And I wouldn't be pressing so hard if you would just sit still."

Sitting still was impossible. My entire body felt as if it wanted to move constantly. My right foot bounced up and down while my left foot twisted back and forth. My right hand twirled a lock of hair around one finger while my left hand rubbed the fabric of my dress.

"You're going to ruin your dress," Mallory scolded me, slapping at my hand. But she didn't sound quite like her usual self, more like she was distracted and unable to put her full effort into criticizing me.

We all weren't quite as focused on getting ready for the dance as we might otherwise have been, if the game hadn't ended like it did. Ackley bringing down Hunter meant the end of the big homecoming game. And a huge victory for Lacede: 27–17.

My chest felt tight and tears threatened to spill down my cheeks whenever I thought of my brother. How was he doing? What was happening at the hospital? Would he be okay?

I tried to push those thoughts aside and sit as still as I could while Elena finished her work on me. "There," she said after a few more moments. "All done."

I looked at myself in the spotty locker-room mirror. The lighting in the room was an unflattering yellow, but still, my cheeks glowed with a rosy color and my lips seemed fuller thanks to the pale lipstick Elena had insisted I wear. I certainly didn't look like myself. Would Greg even recognize me?

My stomach did backflips. I pressed my palms to my abdomen and took a deep breath.

"You look great," Elena said, stepping up behind me. She had gotten ready in half the time of the other girls so that she could help me. Even with doing her makeup and hair quickly, Elena still looked amazing with her smoky eye shadow and dark red lips. Around her neck, a small gold charm was fastened. The charm was a delicate golden apple.

"I can't do this," I whispered. "I feel like I'm going to get sick."

"You'd better not get sick and mess up your lipstick," Elena warned me. "And you *can* do this. Greg is out there, waiting for you. He won't even know what's hit him once he sees you."

"Do you think anyone will be angry that I brought a Spartan as my date?" What I really wanted to ask was, "Am I a traitor to my brother for wanting to be with Greg tonight?"

Hunter's injury had changed things for me. It wasn't just about what I wanted anymore. Almost all my thoughts focused on Hunter. He had tried to get me to stay away from Greg, and I hadn't listened. Had my dream about the game been a warning? Would Hunter be in the boys' locker room right now getting ready for the dance if I had just done what he'd said and ended my friendship with Greg?

"It'll be fine," Elena said. "Perry and I will keep things under control."

I snorted. "That makes me feel *so* relieved."

Elena smiled and pushed me toward the door. "Just shut up and get out there."

My body trembled again as I approached the door. *Calm down*, I told myself. I took in a deep breath and let it out slowly. This was Greg. My Greg. Well, not *my* Greg, but Greg as in my best friend.

With Elena leading the way, I hurried across the school grounds toward the gym.

The lights shone through the glass doors and windows along the front of the building. Students stood on the front steps, the guys trying to look cool and casual while the girls checked out one another's dresses. The low, hushed voices of the crowd and grim expressions on the faces around me echoed the general mood of the evening. It was homecoming, but no one was excited, not after losing to the Spartans and not after what had happened to Hunter.

Elena found Perry quickly and ran off to him, leaving me alone in the courtyard. I scanned the students gathered on the front steps, but there was no sign of Greg. My heartbeat throbbed in my ears. Had I been stood up for my date-that-wasn't-really-a-date-but-that-I-hoped-was-a-date?

"Hey, Cassie."

Greg appeared at my side and I let out the breath I had been holding.

"Hey," I said. He looked great in his dark-gray pants and light-blue shirt, with a gray-and-blue striped tie.

"I didn't know if I should bring a corsage or not," he said, holding up a single white lily. "So I compromised and got this."

I took the lily with a slightly shaky hand. "Thank you," I said, trying to fight back the flush that I knew was creeping up my neck.

Greg offered me his arm. "Ready for our big entrance?" He sounded a little nervous and he glanced warily at the doors of the gym.

I slipped my arm through his, tingling at the warmth of his body through his sleeve. "Ready."

I gave the teachers who attended the doors my dance tickets and they waved us inside. The music already blared throughout the room so that I could feel the vibrations all through my body. The overhead lights had been turned off, with only a few colored spotlights shining. At the far end of the gym hung a huge painted sheet of fabric that proclaimed the theme of the dance with the words TROY HIGH HOMECOMING—HAPPILY EVER AFTER. Along the wall, directly under the sheet, stood the horse float the Spartans had built.

A refreshment table had been set up nearby and students gathered around it. Others danced in the middle of the floor and some sat at small tables along the sides to people-watch.

The mood was strained, but still, as soon as Greg and I entered, I felt the air in the room change. People glanced our way, then turned to whisper to one another. A few people even snickered and sneered.

I considered turning around and leaving, pulling Greg with me. But I didn't want to run away and hide. So I stepped farther into the gym, clutching Greg's arm. We found a small bit of floor space, but immediately everyone cleared away from us.

After a moment, Greg leaned toward me and shouted to be heard over the music, "Do you have any idea what we're supposed to do at a school dance?"

I laughed and relaxed slightly. "I think we're supposed to dance and then drink some punch. But other than that, your guess is as good as mine."

"Okay," Greg said. "Then, do you want to dance?"

I nodded and he led me onto the dance floor. Around us, students jumped and bumped into each other in time with the fast music. We stayed on the edge of the frenzied crowd, just trying to do our own thing. Neither Greg nor I were great dancers, but we had fun doing silly moves to make each other laugh.

After a couple of songs, I got the feeling that more than just a few people were watching us. And it wasn't entirely because of our bad dancing.

I couldn't tell if Greg had noticed. If he had, he did a good job of ignoring it.

"Want to get something to drink?" I asked.

Greg nodded, sweat glistening on his forehead. "Yeah, let's go."

The crowd parted as we moved through, allowing us a clear path to the refreshments. Teachers patrolled the table, I assumed to make sure no one spiked the punch. Greg ladled out two cups of the red drink.

Across the table, Paul Baker and his date, a senior named Jessica, stopped to get some punch. One of them muttered "traitor" as they walked by me.

"What?" I asked, looking at Paul.

He looked up at me, his expression unfriendly. "You heard me. What would Hunter think if he could see his own sister here with the enemy? Especially after we just lost the most important game of the season?"

"Greg doesn't play football," I pointed out.

"He's still a Spartan," Jessica said, scowling at us.

"Hey," Greg said softly. "I'm not here as a Spartan tonight. I want peace between our schools as much as you do. I'm just here to have a good time and let you all see that the Spartans aren't as bad as you think."

Paul snorted. "Go back to Lacede," he growled before turning and marching away.

My face was hot with embarrassment. How could I have thought that bringing Greg here might be a good idea?

"I'm sorry," I said.

"It's not your fault," Greg told me. "It's understandable that people are angry about the game. Hopefully soon everyone will forget about it." He smiled at me, but I didn't feel reassured.

I sipped my drink and faced the dance floor while watching Greg out of the corner of my eye. He drained his drink fast and then stood with the empty cup in his hand, his eyes scanning the crowd but not looking at anything in particular.

He looked stiff and nervous. I should never have asked him to come to this dance. What was I even doing here in the first place? I didn't do school dances. I was not a heels-and-dress kind of girl. And I was crazy for thinking Greg might be with me on an actual *date*. He'd only come because he felt it was his duty as my friend. He probably wished he were with someone else.

I could save us both some embarrassment and frustration by ending the night early.

"Greg—" I said.

But just as I started to speak, he turned to me and said, "I'm going to the bathroom for a minute. Wait here for me, okay?"

I nodded. "Okay."

After Greg disappeared into the crowd, I let my eyes wander over the people on the dance floor. I spotted Elena and Perry dancing close. Elena smiled and looked up at Perry with a peaceful expression on her face. I had never seen her look at Lucas like that.

When Greg returned, I tried to think of something to say to keep us from falling into uncomfortable silence again.

"So . . . the horse is kind of cool," I said, gesturing toward the parade float.

Greg glanced at it, then looked away quickly. "Oh, uh, yeah. I guess we didn't do so bad."

"We?" I asked.

"The student council. Mr. Yancey asked the entire student council to build it, so I helped out a bit. See that front left leg? That's my work. Impressive, huh?"

I laughed. "A work of art. Why didn't you tell me Lacede was doing this?"

"It was supposed to be a surprise," Greg said, not meeting my gaze. He rubbed the back of his neck and looked around nervously.

I couldn't think of anything else to say. It was just the two of us, as it had been so many times before. Only this time was different. This time I was aware of every movement I made, every movement he made. What I wouldn't give to be a mind reader right then. Was he remembering our kiss? Did he want to do it again?

"Cassie," Greg said. He opened his mouth again, but no sound came out. He paused, running a hand through his hair.

I turned toward him. "Yes?"

He lifted his gaze to meet mine. "Cassie," he said again.

"Greg," I said. "Now that we've established each other's names, was there something else you wanted to say?" I squeaked out a laugh, trying to lighten the moment. He was just Greg and I was still just Cassie, his best friend. I didn't want that to change, no matter what else happened between us.

Greg took the tiniest step toward me. "I . . . I've thought . . . I mean, I wanted . . ."

"I guess we know now how Lacede put laxatives in the spaghetti sauce," a voice behind us interrupted.

We spun around, jumping slightly as if we'd been caught doing something wrong. My heart pounded against my ribs as I faced Mallory and Kelsey and the small crowd of cheerleaders behind them.

"What?" I asked Mallory, glaring at her. "What is that supposed to mean?"

"Oh, come on, Cassie." Mallory walked around us

slowly. "The two of you look awfully cozy over here. You claim to be only friends, but it certainly looks like something more than that to rest of us."

My cheeks grew hot. I couldn't look at Greg to see how he reacted to her words.

"Twice now, Lacede has gotten into Troy to play a prank," Mallory continued. "First with the spaghetti and then again with the chickens. I've been wondering just how they're doing it. How are they getting in without anyone noticing?"

"And now we know," Kelsey said. "An insider is helping them."

"I got sick from that spaghetti too," I reminded her. "Why would I eat it if I knew there were laxatives in it?"

"To throw us off your track," said Mallory as she glared at me. "You knew it would make you look less guilty if you were sick like the rest of us."

I rolled my eyes. "Yeah, I'd really make myself sick just to get back at all of you. And as for the chickens—I was in class that morning. Ask Elena. When I walked into the hall, the chickens had already been set loose. How exactly did I let them inside the school while I was in class?"

Mallory looked stumped for a moment, her smile faltering. But then she raised her chin, smiled again, and said, "Why don't *you* tell us?"

I wanted to punch her right in the nose.

"Cassie has had nothing to do with these pranks," Greg said. "You can blame me all you want, but leave her out of it. She's been trying to get everyone to see how stupid they're acting. It might do you some good to listen to her."

Mallory looked back at Greg, one side of her lip curled into a snarl. "Is that a threat, Spartan?"

"No," Greg said. "Just some friendly advice. We're not all bad, you know. If you took the chance to get to know me, you might find that—"

But I didn't hear whatever it was Greg was about to say. Because at that moment, a loud boom thundered throughout the gym and bits of flowers, dust, and wire rained down all around us.

Shrieks filled the air that had clouded with smoke and then someone cried out, "Fire!"

People ran past us, girls holding up their skirts as they ran barefoot and guys slipping on the polished floor in their nice shoes. Someone pushed me backward into Greg, and he caught me to keep me from falling.

"What's going on?" I asked.

The fire alarm suddenly screeched so loudly I could barely hear anything else. I spun around as Greg pulled at my arm. "Come on, Cassie!" he said. "Run!"

At the far end of the gym stood what remained of

the horse parade float—a mess of broken wire frame and burned flowers. Above it, flames licked across the painted banner. The fire spread rapidly over the fabric, moving up the wall toward the strings of lights, paper streamers, and Troy's basketball championship banners.

People pushed past us, their skin coated with dust and debris from the explosion inside the float. Coach Wellens and Ms. Fillmore and a few other members of the Troy High staff stood at the doors, directing students toward the street.

Greg grabbed at me, dragging me along behind him as he moved toward the exit. Once outside, we were nearly separated, but Greg squeezed my hand tight and pulled me closer to him.

"Wait!" I said as something caught my eye.

I stopped at the foot of the headless Trojan statue. Spray-painted across the gray stone were the words SPARTANS WIN.

I stood frozen in place, staring at those blue letters, the paint still wet and dripping, until Greg pulled me away.

"What's going on?" I asked when we reached the street, where the rest of the Trojans had gathered. The stunned faces of my schoolmates surrounded me. Some of the girls cried, huddled together in small groups or wrapped in their boyfriends' arms.

"We have to go, Cassie," Greg said, reaching for my hand. He pushed through the crowd, running down the sidewalk with me in the direction of my house. We moved in silence for several moments.

I felt as if we moved in a dream.

"This wasn't supposed to happen," Greg muttered.

I stopped short, pulling my hand from his grasp. "What do you mean?"

Greg looked as if he were fighting back rage. "Nothing. Let me get you home."

But I stepped back when he reached for me. "What do you mean, Greg?" I asked again through clenched teeth.

Greg stared silently at me.

"You knew about this?" My voice was barely above a whisper. "You knew something was going to happen tonight?"

I knew the answer, but I wanted to hear him say it. I wanted to hear him admit everything to me.

"No," he said. "I mean, yes, I knew something would happen. But it wasn't supposed to be this. Not something dangerous."

I felt as if someone had reached inside my chest and squeezed my heart tight. "You used me."

"No," Greg said, stepping toward me. I stepped back again.

"Yes, you did. You used me to get inside Troy tonight for your stupid prank."

"I didn't, Cassie, I swear! Some guys snuck into the gym before the game ended so they could rig the float to explode at a certain time."

"So they could burn down my school?" I shouted. The wail of sirens echoed in the distance. "Someone could have gotten hurt."

"No!" Greg's face contorted into a deep frown. "It was only supposed to be a small explosion to send the flowers shooting off in the air, you know, just to give a little scare. I don't know what happened. I would never have agreed to an explosion that could cause a fire."

I choked back a sob as I looked into his eyes. He wasn't the Greg I knew.

"Go home," I said.

"Cassie—"

I picked up a rock from the road and threw it at him. He ducked, and it sailed over his shoulder.

"Go away," I told him.

"Cassie, listen to me," Greg pleaded.

"No!" I shouted as tears fell down my cheeks. "I hate you! I never want to see you again!"

I turned and started running back toward school, toward the people I belonged with. But Greg's arms suddenly circled my waist, pulling me back to him. I turned around and pushed at his chest, trying to get away.

And then Greg pressed his lips to mine.

For a moment, I felt as if I were melting. My legs grew weak and I wouldn't have been able to stay standing if Greg hadn't still held on to me.

But he lied to me. He knew the Spartans had planned something bad and he wasn't going to say a word. He let me believe he really wanted to be at the dance with me when in reality he just came to make sure everything was in place for Lacede's final prank on Troy.

I pushed him away as hard as I could and ran toward Troy High burning in the distance.

27

"POLICE ARE INVESTIGATING THE CAUSE OF LAST night's fire at Troy High School, which happened during the school's homecoming dance. As of now, police have not named a suspect. If you know any information, please call the Troy Police Department at—"

I turned off the TV. I couldn't stand to listen to any more news reports about what had happened at Troy.

After I'd left Greg, I had run back to where everyone else still stood in the road. The fire had spread quickly, engulfing all the paper decorations and the float, and smoke billowed out of the gym. Even from a distance, the smoke burned my eyes. At least I could blame my watery eyes on that if anyone asked any questions.

I had moved through the crowd unnoticed, so I was

able to take a good look at my schoolmates. Mallory and Kelsey sat on the asphalt, visibly shaken. Some of the guys from the football team watched the flames and muttered under their breaths about Spartans. And nearby, Perry held a trembling Elena in his arms.

Hunter should have been there. He would have known what to do. He would have been able to make us do something, anything other than just stand there looking lost and bewildered as we watched our school burn.

But Ackley had made sure that Hunter wasn't there with us. Maybe that had been the plan all along. Take out Hunter, and Troy would fall.

The fire department and police had arrived quickly. While the firefighters worked on putting out the flames, the police officers ushered us down the street and away from the school. Everyone started calling their parents and soon cars squealed to a stop in the road and panicked parents rushed over to us.

Mom and Dad were with Hunter at the hospital, so I wasn't sure whether to call them or not. I found Perry and Elena again and asked, "What should we do?"

"I just called Dad," Perry told me. "Come on, I'm taking both of you home."

I curled up on the couch when we got there. As much as I wanted to stop it, I dreamed of Greg. I dreamed of his lips on mine and melting in his arms as the fire raged around us.

I heard the front door open and I sat up, rubbing at my eyes.

"Anyone home?" Dad called.

"In here," I called back.

Dad came through the doorway, followed by Mom and Hunter. Mom held tightly to Hunter's left hand. His right arm, from wrist to shoulder, had been wrapped in bandages and was held in place with a sling.

"Are you okay?" I asked, jumping up and hurrying toward my brother.

"We'll see," Hunter said. "The doctor says I have a separated shoulder. Nothing to do now but wait and see how I heal." He grimaced slightly.

"We lost to the Spartans," he added somberly.

"Do you need anything, honey?" Mom asked. She grabbed a throw pillow and fluffed it before stuffing it under Hunter's arm. "Do you want a sandwich? Something to drink?"

"I'm fine," Hunter said. "Really, Mom. I just want to sit down for a little while. I don't need anything."

"What about you, Cassie?" Mom asked, turning to me.

"I'm okay," I said.

"Okay." Mom stepped back, wringing her hands.

"Come on, Mary," Dad said. "We've been up all night. Let's get some sleep."

After my parents left, I studied my brother for a moment as he sat there with his eyes closed. He didn't look like a leader right then. He looked broken, weak, and vulnerable. He looked just like everyone else who walked the halls of Troy High.

"Don't worry about Ackley," I said as I sat down on the couch. "I promise he'll get what's coming to him."

"He will," Hunter agreed. "But not from you."

"I'm not a weak little kid," I said.

The look of anger on my brother's face surprised me. "You are so stupid sometimes. Just stay out of it, Cassie."

For a moment, I couldn't breathe. Hunter had never talked to me like that before.

"I'm just trying to help you out," I said, clenching my fists in my lap. "And I can't stand the thought of Ackley thinking he's won this war."

"The Spartans did win," Hunter said, sounding exhausted. "We lost the game, Troy burned, and I'm in these bandages for who knows how long. The war is over and Troy is defeated." He rubbed at his eyes with his left hand. "I don't want to talk about this anymore, Cassie. Just stay away from Ackley and those other guys. You should never have been involved in this battle."

I stood, but I didn't leave just yet. I glared down at my brother and said, "You're not the only one who lost here, you know. You may have lost some stupid fight with the Spartans, but I lost my best friend. For *you*. So don't tell me this wasn't my fight too."

"Cassie—"

But I hurried out of the room before Hunter could say anything else.

28

"HEY, CASSIE." ELENA PLOPPED DOWN ONTO THE couch next to me on Sunday afternoon. Perry sat down on her other side, slipping his arm around her shoulder.

"Hey," I answered. I wasn't in the mood for visitors. I had been sitting on the couch, watching some old movie on TV. Well, I wasn't really watching it. I was just staring at the screen.

Earlier, Mom had insisted I eat something. I had managed to eat a few spoonfuls of tomato soup, but that was all that I could force down. My stomach felt hollow. So did my chest. Everything felt hollow.

I had been avoiding Hunter ever since our argument the day before. I didn't want to see him. Every time I looked at him, I just thought about Greg. What exactly had this entire war between our schools accomplished? Nothing that I could see, other than the fact that Troy High would have no usable gym for the next few months.

It had been a complete waste of time and energy. And now I'd lost Greg.

"The basketball team is really mad about the gym," Elena told me. "We just ran into a couple of the guys from the team at the mall. They heard that the gym won't be completely repaired until after basketball season is over. So that means any home games we have scheduled will have to be held somewhere else. People are saying Lacede is the most likely place, since it's the closest school to Troy."

I snorted. "How ironic."

"Yeah," Perry muttered. "Lacede destroys our gym and now we have to use theirs."

"This really doesn't seem like something Lucas would think up," Elena said. "He's not that clever. If anyone's behind it, I bet it's Ackley. He's always struck me as kind of crazy, like he would do anything to protect his pride. Anyway," she went on, turning to me, "how is Greg doing?"

Perry stiffened.

I shrugged. "I wouldn't know. Greg and I aren't friends anymore."

"It's about time," Perry said.

Elena elbowed him in the ribs. "Shut up." She looked at me, frowning. "What do you mean?"

"We were never meant to be friends," I said. "He's a Spartan and I'm a Trojan."

"So?"

I couldn't believe what I was hearing. "So, the last three months our schools have been fighting a huge war against each other. Or have you not noticed?"

Elena rolled her eyes. "Of course I noticed. But what does that have to do with you and Greg? You two are made for each other. I don't know why it's taken you so long to figure that out. I could see it the first time I met you at Greg's house."

I shook my head. "We're just friends. Or we were."

"Don't try to lie to me, Cassie," Elena said. "I'm your fake best friend, remember?"

I laughed a little at that.

"You and Greg understand each other," Elena continued. "And believe me, it's hard to find a guy who always remembers your favorite ice-cream flavor."

"Hey," Perry said. "I take offense to that!"

Elena raised her eyebrows at him. "Oh, really? What's my favorite flavor then?"

Perry looked stumped for a moment. Then he grinned and said, "Strawberry."

"Wrong." Elena turned back to me. "See, Cassie? When you find the right guy, you have to hold on to him. And my favorite flavor is rocky road," she told Perry.

"I was close!" Perry protested.

"How is strawberry even remotely close to rocky road?" Elena asked.

Perry leaned toward her and nuzzled her cheek. "They're both sweet. Like you."

Elena giggled and kissed him.

It was a good thing I didn't have anything in my stomach to throw up at the sight of them.

"Okay," I said, "so maybe I like Greg. But that doesn't mean he likes me back."

I tried not to think about the way he'd kissed me. It must have just been something to distract me from the fire.

"Oh, please," Elena said, breaking away from Perry's lips long enough to speak. "Why do you think he hasn't had a girlfriend during the entire two years you've been friends?"

Before I could answer her, Perry pulled her toward him again.

29

THE NEXT WEEK PASSED IN A FOG. I GOT UP, went to school, came home, did my homework, went to bed, and started the routine over again the next day. I barely noticed that the mood around school seemed to be pretty somber. The gym had been roped off and no one was allowed near it, so it sat empty and blackened. Most people tried not to look at it as they walked around campus. No one even sat in the courtyard anymore, so the headless Trojan and his horse stood alone. At least now the spray paint had been cleaned off.

I could get through most days without speaking more than five words to anyone. Elena filled the silence with her constant chatter.

But still, no one seemed to notice that I had fallen

into a sort of depression. Nothing made me happy. It was like the entire world meant nothing to me anymore. I felt more alone and invisible than I ever had before Elena came to Troy.

On Saturday afternoon, I was lying on my stomach on my bed, one arm dangling off the side of the mattress, when there was a knock on my door.

I didn't answer, but the door opened after a moment anyway.

Hunter leaned against the door frame, looking in at me. "Hey, Cassie."

I turned my head so that I faced the wall. I didn't have the energy to talk to anyone, especially Hunter.

The sound of footsteps moved across the room to my bed. I could feel him standing there, looking down at me. It had been more than a week since we'd said even one word to each other.

"What do you want?" I finally asked, unable to stand his silence any longer.

"I came to give you something," Hunter said.

"I don't want anything from you," I mumbled.

"Tough," Hunter said. "Just humor me for five minutes. If you still hate me after that, I won't ever bother you again."

I sighed, but I sat up and looked at my brother. His right arm was still in a sling, strapped tightly to his body.

I had overheard Mom and Dad saying one night how worried they were about whether his separated shoulder would fully heal. Hunter would very likely need surgery soon and his future football career depended on how successfully his shoulder could be repaired.

"I'm really sorry, Cassie," Hunter began.

I crossed my arms and turned my head to the side. I wasn't going to forgive him with just one little apology.

"I've been so stupid lately," he continued. "I don't blame you for not wanting to talk. I wish I could go back and change everything I've done over the last couple of months."

I turned to look at him, but still didn't say anything.

Hunter paced back and forth across my room, running his good hand through his hair. "I got so caught up in football and this rivalry. I wanted to leave my mark on Troy by making a big difference in my senior year. You know? I wanted to be this person who kids would talk about for years. The guy who finally put an end to the rivalry by rallying everyone behind him and destroying Lacede on the field. I mean, what else have I done to be remembered for?"

"You're a great football player," I said. "People will remember you for that."

"No, they won't," Hunter said. "I wanted to become a

big football star who everyone would remember went to Troy High. But it's more than just football. I wanted to be remembered as the guy who finally ended this fifty-year rivalry. I wanted everyone to know my name."

"There are other things more important in life than being remembered by a bunch of high school kids," I said.

"I know," Hunter said, laughing a little. "I've been really, really stupid these last couple of months. I'm just as much to blame for what's happened as Perry and Elena, or the Spartans. Maybe even more so." He sat on the edge of my bed and looked over his shoulder at me. "But I never meant for you to get hurt, Cassie. I swear."

"I know." I leaned forward, wrapping my arms carefully around his shoulders.

Hunter smiled sadly. "Good. Because I just might be stuck here next year if my shoulder doesn't heal and I can't play football."

"You'll play again," I said, although I wasn't exactly sure that was true.

Hunter stood and held out his left hand toward me. "Come on. There's something for you downstairs."

I followed my brother down the stairs, wondering what it was he wanted to give me.

Hunter led me into the den and then stepped back, grinning wide.

Greg was sitting on our couch. Martial Battle 2 was paused on the TV screen in front of him.

He stood when he saw us enter, but he didn't make a move toward me. Instead, he shoved his hands into his pockets and looked down at the floor, as if he were nervous.

I looked at Hunter, but I couldn't speak because of the huge lump in my throat that felt as if I'd swallowed a sock.

"I'm sorry for everything I've put you through, Cassie," Hunter said. "I've finally figured out that there are more important things in life than football." He smiled at me, squeezed my hand, and then left the room.

Greg and I stood facing each other silently for a long time.

Finally, I said the first thing that came to mind.

"I'm sorry about that embarrassing picture of you at Lacede."

Greg looked startled, then he laughed. "Well, I can always get you back for that, you know. I have plenty of embarrassing pictures of you. Remember when you dressed up like Michael Jackson for Halloween?"

A laugh escaped before I could force it back down. I wanted to be mad at him, but I couldn't. I had missed him so much, and the sight of him there in my house thrilled me.

"I'm sorry this all got out of hand," Greg said. "I never meant for it to come between us."

"I'm sorry too," I said. "I was a part of it just like you were."

"Seriously, Cassie," Greg said, taking a few steps toward me. "I didn't know the Spartans were going to set the gym on fire. The explosion was supposed to be small and harmless. But someone else convinced them to change things behind my back."

"Ackley?" I asked.

Greg nodded. "I think so. I have no proof and the guys aren't saying anything, but I bet it was him."

"Okay," I said, "then tell me about the laxatives in the spaghetti sauce. I have to know how you pulled that off."

Greg gave me a mischievous grin. "Cassie, think about it. Fifty former Lacede students now walk the halls of Troy High. And not all of them switched their allegiances as quickly as Elena."

I laughed. "Okay, fair enough." I was quiet for a moment, then said, "I'm sorry I messed up our friendship."

Greg blinked, looking confused. "How did you mess it up?"

"You know," I said, unable to meet his gaze. "By kissing you that day."

I snuck a glance at Greg and saw that his face had

reddened. "I know you hated it," I said, "and it's made things weird between us and I'm sorry—"

"Cassie," Greg said. "First of all, I didn't hate it. And the only reason it's made things weird is because I wanted to kiss you again, but when I finally did, you pushed me away!"

I blinked at him, unable to say anything.

"I've liked you ever since I first saw you at band camp," Greg said, moving toward me. "Why else would I have sat down in that closet after you attacked me with ice cream? But you've always seemed interested in only being my friend. I didn't want to do anything to mess things up between us either. Then you kissed me and I couldn't figure out what was going on." He scowled. "Have I ever mentioned how annoying you girls are? How are guys supposed to figure out anything when you're always giving us mixed signals?"

The room felt as if it were spinning around me. I was so busy trying to make sense of everything Greg had just said that I didn't notice him moving closer until he stood just inches away from me.

"So why did you kiss me?" he asked in a low voice.

"I—I don't know," I stammered. My legs shook and my palms were wet with sweat. I didn't want to mess things up again.

But then I realized some risks were worth taking.

"Cassie," Greg said, "will you just kiss me again?"

I smiled. "The last time we kissed, we started a war."

"That wasn't our war," Greg said. "And now it's over. It's just you and me. The only war I'm interested in is our ongoing video-game battles. And by the way, I am totally going to kick your butt."

"That's what you think," I told him.

I pulled Greg to me before he could say anything else. And kissed my best friend once again.

AUTHOR'S NOTE

Troy High was inspired by the story of the Trojan War and Helen of Troy. I hope that readers familiar with Homer's *Iliad* will be able to pick out the similarities in the storylines, but you don't have to be an expert in Greek mythology to enjoy the story itself!

There are many more characters in *The Iliad* than I included in *Troy High*, but I had to drastically condense the main characters to keep from turning this story into an epic of its own. Here's a list of the characters in *Troy High* and their Trojan War counterparts:

Cassie Prince—Cassandra the Seer, princess of Troy

Greg Mennon—Agamemnon, brother of Menelaus, commander in chief of the Greeks

Perry Prince—Paris, prince of Troy

Hunter Prince—Hector, the finest warrior and prince of Troy

Elena Argos—Helen of Troy, the greatest beauty and wife of Menelaus

Lucas Mennon—Menelaus, brother of Agamemnon,
first husband of Helen, and king of Sparta

Owen—Odysseus

Ackley—Achilles

Patrick—Patrocles

This was the hardest and most enjoyable book I've written. A *lot* of research went into it, not only on the Trojan War itself, but also on individual characters in the story, American high school football, and high school rivalries. But I had a lot of fun learning more about mythology and thinking of the pranks that the schools could play on each other.

I decided to write a modern-day retelling of the Trojan War because I've loved Greek mythology since I first began learning about it in the seventh grade. I love reading about the gods and goddesses and the ancient heroes that appear in the stories. The Helen of Troy story in particular has interested me. I always wondered how Helen felt, being taken from her home and family and then having so many people die while trying to win her back. How did all the other people who found themselves sucked into the battle feel? I always knew I wanted to tell my own story about Helen of Troy, but it wasn't until I started plotting out *Troy High* that I figured out how I wanted to tell it. The story of the war between these two groups of people seemed ideal to twist into a story involving high school rivalry, popularity, and romance. The football field was the perfect modern-day battlefield. And who hasn't thought about the many Helens who roamed the hallways of her own high school?

I decided to tell the story from Cassie's point of view instead of Elena's because Cassie was close enough to the action to be a part of everything, yet removed enough to see the disaster that's looming ahead when Elena arrives at Troy. Cassandra the Seer was cursed—she could see the future, but no one would ever believe her. In *Troy High*, Cassie has a bit of a premonition that things won't end well, but of course, her brothers and friends brush her warnings aside because they're so focused on what they think is right.

I did take a few liberties with the story in my retelling to suit a modern high school setting. One of the biggest differences is the relationship between Cassie and Greg. After the fall of Troy, when the Greeks ransacked the city, they took Trojan women as concubines to take back home with them. Agamemnon chose Cassandra. It was not a match made of romance, but the relationship was the basis for Cassie's friendship and romance with Greg. Of course, their story has a much happier ending than the one about Agamemnon and Cassandra!

ACKNOWLEDGMENTS

I couldn't have done *Troy High* alone. Many, many thanks to my editor, Tamar Brazis, for believing in this story and helping me turn the idea into the final product. I don't think I could ever say thank you enough to my agent, Stephen Barbara, for everything he's done and the support he's given me.

Huge thanks to the best critique partners—Marlene Perez, Emily Marshall, and Sandra Delisle!

Thanks to my seventh-grade English teacher, Ms. Spence, who made us study Greek mythology and sparked my love for *The Iliad*.

And of course, thanks to Homer—the poet, not the cartoon character—who told the story of the Trojan War and inspired me to tell it my own way.

Always, a thousand thanks to my family and friends for their support.

ABOUT THE AUTHOR

Shana Norris is the author of *Something to Blog About*. She knew from a young age that she wanted to be a writer. Well, actually, she wanted to be a ballerina, an archaeologist, a teacher, *and* a writer. But after she realized that she'd never taken a ballet lesson in her life, she didn't like to get dirty, and she hated being in a classroom all day, she decided to be a writer. She lives in Kinston, North Carolina, with her husband and their dogs, Chloe and Daisy, as well as three lazy cats named Elmo, Callie, and Bandit. This is her second novel. Please visit www.shananorris.com.

This book was designed by Maria T. Middleton and art directed by Chad W. Beckerman. The text is set in 12-point FF Celeste, a typeface designed by typographer and type historian Chris Burke in 1994. The display type is Boton and Lithos.

KEEP READING!

The Girls
By TUCKER SHAW

◆ ◆ ◆

978-0-8109-8348-9 • U.S. $16.95 hardcover
978-0-8109-8991-7 • U.S. $6.95 paperback

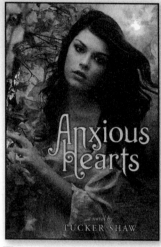

Anxious Hearts
By TUCKER SHAW

◆ ◆ ◆

978-0-8109-8718-0 • U.S. $16.95 hardcover

Something to Blog About
By SHANA NORRIS

◆ ◆ ◆

978-0-8109-9474-4
U.S. $15.95 hardcover